CHICAGO SHORTS

MIKE WALKER

Copyright © 2013 by Mike Walker

ISBN 978-0-7414-8101-6 Paperback
ISBN 978-0-7414-8191-7 eBook

Printed in the United States of America

This is a work of non-fiction with fictional embellishments.

Published January 2013

INFINITY PUBLISHING
1094 New DeHaven Street, Suite 100
West Conshohocken, PA 19428-2713
Toll-free (877) BUY BOOK
Local Phone (610) 941-9999
Fax (610) 941-9959
Info@buybooksontheweb.com
www.buybooksontheweb.com

CONTENTS

INTRODUCTIONS

Each of us has a story, and each of us likely thinks ours is interesting. Childhood plays a key role in who we become as adults, but it's not until we become adults and look back on our past that we acknowledge what our childhood really meant. How we define it, rationalize it, and resolve it is critically important to our lives. *Chicago Shorts* helped me put my childhood into perspective, and to bring a new understanding to a life already lived. We can drive away from our past, but our childhood and our hometowns will always be in our review mirrors no matter how far we travel. For me this view in hindsight is, well, pretty bizarre.

I read a lot of books as an English major at Western Illinois University, but the novels were hard to get through. I mean, who has time to work through 300 pages when there are so many other things to do? Contemporary technology has shortened our span of attention to the length of a sound byte—an infomercial, an email, a text, a tweet.

I've always had a fondness for short stories. You can get through them quickly, and they require that the writer get to the point. My favorite is Jack London's *To Build a Fire*. Some might say I have a sick sense of humor, and certainly the vision of a guy freezing his ass off on the frozen tundra of the Yukon Trail while desperately trying to build a fire to stay alive isn't for everyone.

After the main character finally gets the fire going and thinks he's made it, having outsmarted the old codger who earlier told him it was too cold to go out on the frozen trail that day, the fire is extinguished by an avalanche of snow descending from the branches of a pine tree above. He built the fire in the wrong spot. A simple error in placement, just a few yards difference, was enough to doom the man. In a last ditch attempt to save himself, he tries to kill his dog and climb inside its body for warmth. The dog, like the old man who forecast the main character's demise, was just plain smarter than the clumsy man, and runs away to seek what the man could no longer provide: shelter and food. So the story ends with the man in a manic state, flailing his arms about and running along a creek bed in the middle of nowhere, totally mad and keenly aware he is about to freeze to death. And the last thought in his mind was that the speculative, grey-bearded old timer who warned him it was too cold to hike alone that day was *right*. I love the simple lessons London provides his readers in *To Build a Fire*: life has a sick sense of humor, and sometimes we really are our own worst enemies.

Chicago Shorts is a book of short stories based on real experiences with real characters. People I knew, experiences I had, places I've been while growing up in the south suburbs of Chicago. Fictional embellishments were added to emphasize the significance of my experiences. Some of the names of people from my past have been left unchanged; others have been changed to save me the time of asking people I haven't spoken to in twenty years permission to use their name in a book. I'm not worried about saving them embarrassment. Each of us must own our experiences, our mistakes, our foibles. But they'll read the stories and know who I'm talking about. Trust me, no one has more to account for about their past than I. If anything in the book offends the people mentioned, my apologies. I'm not stating facts from my past, just providing my interpretation of what happened. If my version is different from others,' then I'll have proven what we already know: that memory is a subjective thing. But for the characters mentioned herein who may have repressed their childhood delinquencies, you have me to thank for conjuring them back.

Since I wasn't sure exactly how to kick things off, I created three different introductions to *Chicago Shorts*. Read them and pick the one you like the best, then try to forget about the other two and continue reading the book. Thanks for checking out *Chicago Shorts*.

Intro #1

I began writing this book when I turned 40. Figuring I may live to be around 80, I thought I might as well reflect on my life at the halfway point. It's not that I've traveled the world—I've never been outside the continental United States other than Hawaii, once—or that I have great wisdom to bestow. I'm living proof that with a little hard work and luck, anyone can be successful. But I've experienced some things that are at least interesting, if not entertaining, if not totally peculiar; the pages that follow are an account of some of my more memorable and meaningful childhood experiences. Some of these experiences and their descriptions will seem quippy, but the themes of Chicago Shorts—small town America, racism, teenage wonderment and mischief, rebellion and loss—will evolve as you progress through the book. I hope they impact you as they have me. Augusten Burroughs may have run with scissors when he was a kid, but I was right next to him running on glass in bare feet.

Intro #2

I'm a typical type-A over-achiever who keeps life in a certain order and makes good on most of the goals I establish for myself. I also try to live life according to the Latin phrase *temet nosce*: "know thyself." But a certain paradox exists in the very concept of getting to know oneself. Most people may believe they can objectively look at themselves with a critical lens; however, the intrinsic bias and defense mechanisms that possess us make it near impossible to do this to any legitimate or successful degree. The older we get, the less we are capable of being anything other than who we are wired to be. The coolest people I know are the ones who understand this and are okay with it.

Anyway, I just can't walk into bookstores anymore and look at thousands of books written by authors, lawyers, doctors, housewives, average Joes, and the guy down the block who "quit work to become a writer," and believe that they have something more interesting to offer in print than I do. If I'm wrong, there aren't many of you reading this book right now anyway. If I'm right, I may just be able to send my daughters to good colleges after all.

Intro #3

As I alluded to in my reference to London's *To Build a Fire*, life has a sick sense of humor. Know before you read this book who I am as a person, akin to the necessity of getting to know a political candidate before you vote for him or her. Even though I had the pleasure of meeting and having lunch with Tau Kappa Epsilon fraternity brother Ronald Reagan in 1990, the first president I voted for was Barack Obama. I voted for President Obama not just because of his ties to Chicago (he was there only briefly), but because he speaks with genuine enthusiasm about America and how to get it back on track.

It seems appropriate for you to know a little more about the author of the book you purchased (assuming you actually purchased a copy and not that I gave you one. If a copy was given to you, I really don't owe you the same courtesy. If you're a friend of mine, whether you purchased your copy or not, you already know me, so you can skip the rest of intro number three altogether).

In college I told my parents I was a liberal just to annoy them and to rebel against them and Dolton's conservative mindset. I don't currently classify myself as a staunch liberal, but "liberal-minded." It wasn't just attending college that formed my liberal outlook. I know a lot of highly conservative college graduates. Possibly it was listening to my favorite band Rush during my formative years. I not only wanted to play drums like Neil Peart, I wanted to be a "New World Man" just like the song, tasting everything that life offered and accomplishing every goal I set for myself. A Renaissance Man. I've always been a big *carpe diem* enthusiast, believing that every day is a gift we should cherish and make the most of. This mentality still drives my work ethic and optimistic outlook on people and life. We're only on this merry-go-round once, so we might as well enjoy the ride.

When I was growing up everyone envied Jay Boros, the kid with the big house and in-ground swimming pool, billiards table and fireplace, whose parents drove a Lincoln Continental. These were luxuries almost no one in my hometown of Dolton had. I decided back then that if I worked hard I too could have these things. Even liberal-minded people should be able to enjoy their version of the American Dream, right?

Working on college campuses for twenty years has made me a kinder, more compassionate person. Most of my values are aligned with the values of others who may call themselves liberals, a dirty word in many pockets of society including the south suburbs of Chicago where I grew up, but a celebrated word on most college campuses where I have worked my entire life since leaving Chicago. Treating people differently because of their gender, sexual orientation, skin color, or religion never made sense to me. Life is too short to believe we are better than the next person. When we become capable of lowering our defenses against those who are most different from us, we stand to learn a lot and experience some really enlightening moments.

I believe the government should do its best to maintain democracy, ensure basic personal freedoms, protect its citizenry, and advance capitalism as a social and economic model while leveling the playing field so that every citizen has a chance to be successful, enjoy life, and embrace whatever they define as their "American Dream." But I also know successful people who are miserable, so I don't necessarily treat success and happiness as synonyms.

I am fervently pro-choice, and believe if two people love each other they should be able to be together, in matrimony or other civil unions, whether they are the same or opposite sex. Let's face it, with today's divorce rate, I'm not sure why gay couples want to rush into marriage anyway, other than perhaps deserving the label as much as heterosexual couples, and to enjoy the health care and tax benefits that come with marriage. But making marriage last is hard work, and I'm one of the lucky few who still finds it cool when my wife says to someone, "This is my husband."

I believe that people of all color, religions, shapes, and abilities should be treated equally, and that we should jealously care for our environment before we destroy it any more than we already have. So I guess all this makes me a "moderate, non-card-carrying liberal democrat" (I say non-card carrying because I am luke warm on politics in general, accept as friends people of all political persuasions, and am not about recruiting people to believe as I believe or vote as I vote. To each his own). I appreciate that some find this label an oxymoron. Sorry. There are moderate liberals who eat red meat, befriend those in the NRA, and just want everyone to get along. Kum-bay-a.

So *Chicago Shorts* is a series of short stories that, when pieced together, define the life of an average American who worked hard to be successful, got a few breaks along the way, saw some crazy, funny—if not ironic—and provocative stuff, and learned not to take life too seriously. Most mornings I wake up and ask myself, ala David Byrne of the Talking Heads, "Well, how did I get here?" I'm amazingly lucky to have the wife, kids, and job that I do. I've had a great adulthood and a great childhood. *Chicago Shorts* represents the bridge that merges my youth and my current recollection of my youth. I hope you find the stories much like life itself...funny, tragic and beautiful.

INSPIRATIONS

To the two best women on the planet- Barbie Eisenhauer
and BettyAnn Walker. You influence my life every day.

To Dad- *Black Beauty* is a metaphor for your life.
You embody kindness, sympathy and respect.

To Cassidy and Kendall- Being your dad completes me. Respect
your art and everything else will evolve around you.

To Jimmy Throw, Eddy Hoekstra, Todd Bergfors and
Billy Miklos- RIP. See you guys on the dark side of the moon.

To Jim Morgan, Terry Kane, Paul Lamb, Nick Misch, Jay Boros,
Kurt Graf, Tony Jurgeto, Jimmy Gorombei, Danny Rambeaux,
Kenny Tatina, Scott Edwards, Stevie Guzak, Randy Wojtas, Will
Svilar and Johnnie Hahn- Being a kid with you guys was a wild ride.
Ish Kabibble lives.

To Standard Deviation- Still rockin' after all these years.

To the Walker Brothers- Let's just try
to make it out of this life alive.

ACKNOWLEDGEMENTS

Thank you to Haley Forbush Weldon for reviewing my
initial draft, and to Erica Sklar for editing the text.

Thank you to Teresa Kramer for the amazing cover illustrations.
You banana!

WELCOME TO DOLTON, ILLINOIS

Let me tell you of the idealism of small town suburbia, a great place to be a kid. Now help me roll it over and show you its underbelly, the barnacles of racism we were bound and blind to until the big city saved us, liberating us from the shackles of our little town...

The second oldest of four boys, I was raised in a single income family from a modest south suburb of Chicago—Dolton, Illinois. Dolton doesn't appear on most maps nor is it mentioned in many sophisticated conversations about politics, celebrities or much else. Perhaps the biggest sources of pride for Dolton were hosting President Jimmy Carter for a town hall meeting in 1979, and our high school, Thornridge, winning the Illinois State High School Basketball Championships in 1971 and '72. The 1972 team, arguably the best Illinois high school basketball team ever, beat Quincy in the championship game by an impressive margin of 104-69.

One of my earliest childhood memories was getting excused early from Vandenberg Elementary so all the kids could go home to watch the title games on their little black and white televisions. Those two years the team set a new state record for consecutive wins, and sent a previously unknown black kid named Quinn Buckner to Indiana University on an athletic scholarship, where he was co-captain of their 1976 national championship team. Quinn later won an NBA championship with the 1984 Boston Celtics, and is one of only three basketball players to win championships at the high school, college, and professional levels.

In the 1980s Kevin Duckworth graduated from T'Ridge, played basketball for Eastern Illinois University and then for the NBA Portland Trailblazers. "Duck" was a two-time NBA All-Star and on the team that lost to Michael Jordan and the Chicago Bulls in the NBA championship in 1992. An enormous physical specimen and gifted athlete, Duck eclipsed most other kids as he walked the school's hallways. Our head basketball coach, Mr. Kennedy, used to drive to his house in nearby Harvey at 5am, wake him up and make him run off some of the pounds he needed to lose in order to even be considered for a division one basketball scholarship. Coach Kennedy's inspiration and mentoring of Duck worked. Chants of "WE ARE T.R." carried over and echoed in Duck's ears all through his stellar college career at Eastern Illinois University, where he was team co-MVP and first team all-conference during the 1985-'86 season; he still holds the EIU school record for career blocks and rebounds. Other than these basketball greats, a few other notables emerged from the Dolton streets.

Jane Lynch, star of the hit television show Glee, graduated from Thornridge in 1977. Actors Michael and Virginia Madsen weren't raised in Dolton, but hung out at the Izaak Walton club. Richard Roeper emerged from Thornridge to find success as a notable film critic, teaming with Roger Ebert on "At the Movies" after Gene Siskel died. I met Roeper, quite the celebrity, at the Chicago Marriot in 2011 after he gave a keynote address, walked up to him and said, "Nice to meet you. I went to Thornridge High." "Go Falcons," was his only reply, not stopping to shake my hand or make eye contact. He walked off the stage, mingled for thirty seconds, then left with an entourage of several gorgeous women at his side. Sorry to sound like Holden Caulfield, but what a phony.

Like most other Chicago suburbs, in the 1950s Dolton was an idyllic little community with cute houses, proud residents, good schools and beautiful little parks and playgrounds, where hard working, mostly white families emerging from Chicago eagerly moved to start a new life. Dolton rests on Chicago's southern border, around a 20 minute drive from its inner city.

Growing up, all my friends' parents said they came from an area of Chicago called "Roseland," and left there to move to Dolton because Roseland was "ruined by the blacks." My parents bought our two-level, 2,000 square foot home for $19,000 in 1965. All brick, three bedrooms, one and half baths, and an unfinished basement—for them, the American Dream fulfilled. The same dream was being fulfilled for most Dolton residents.

Every residential street in Dolton looked pretty much the same: eight or ten houses with detached garages and small back yards separated by chain link fences—fences that marked property lines and divided each symmetrical, rectangular lot, but which also united neighbors. Fences we leaned on to exchange simple conversations with the family next door, short enough to hand over an extra box of pasta or a can of corn to lend a hand to a neighbor who didn't make it to the grocery store that day, or a tool to fix something, or a bowl of homemade soup if one of the kids had the flu. Fencing visible from both sides, making each family's existence transparent. Conversations were audible from yard to yard, so your business was everyone's. And when neighbors weren't barbequing in their backyards, they were sitting on their front porches, also known as "stoops," with other neighbors, talking over coffee or an Old Style beer, directing the kids to fetch another as the adults tried to unwind from their blue collar work days.

Dolton was a great place to grow up. It was Rockwellian in every way. Long before the Internet, the streets of Dolton were ours, and we[1] passed our time riding our bikes all over town. We barely stopped for lunch, and weren't distracted by the later developed intrusions of 300 cable channels, the Internet, or cell phones. As a general rule, when the street lights came on it was time to go home. But this left us hours and hours to explore, catch garter snakes behind Dolton Boys baseball fields, to head to Kmart and pester the truck drivers loading soda on the docks for a free bottle of Canfields, or to climb to the top of L Fish Furniture and survey the town from its rooftop (and later to bring girls and beer up there where the cops couldn't see us).

We checked out the latest motocross bikes at Mr. Ed's Bike Shop, and always stopped to buy a bag of candy from Panazzo's corner store. I mowed neighbors' lawns or shoveled snow off their walkways for $2 per house, mostly to earn money for a trip to Dolton Bowling Alley to play Pacman, Asteroids, Space Invaders, or to bowl a few games. Extra money also meant stopping at Dunkin Donuts to flirt with the teenage waitresses, or for lunch at Dog & Suds or Cal's Roast Beef. On weekends we hung out at Wright's Arcade Barnyard in South Holland trying to look cool. And the first week of every July meant the Dolton Volunteer Firefighters' parade,

---

[1] I use the collective "we" in *Chicago Shorts* to include my friends and my three brothers.

3

carnival, and fireworks. The amusement rides, the games and prizes, the big red fire engines with blaring sirens rolling in the parade and the fireworks show were the highlight of every kid's summer. When we didn't have distractions such as the annual carnival to keep us busy we found our own excitement, and the winter months provided a host of options.

Chicago winters are long, cold, and gray. The first snow of the season is as beautiful as the last snow of the season is dreadful. And sometimes it snows heavy, what Chicagoans call "lake-effect snow," given Dolton's proximity to Lake Michigan. During the heaviest snowfalls Wiseway Foods paid us cash to push the shopping carts through the deep snow in the parking lot back into the store. Five bucks an hour seemed like a fortune then. But Chicago winters brought lots of outdoor activities for kids—sledding, skating, playing hockey, building snow forts and snowmen, and having snowball fights were among our favorite winter games. Less sensible, but measurably more fun, activities included "skeeching" behind cars by grabbing onto the rear bumper while the car is in motion, and off-roading cars through the snow in Kandy Kane Park.

How our parents never suspected us of being trouble-makers is hard to tell. They probably figured as long as we weren't selling drugs or holding up liquor stores, everything else could slide. We were part of the American Dream our parents believed in—a house in the suburbs with kids. Accepting that any of these three elements were anything less than perfect would equate to admitting the Dream wasn't all it was cracked up to be. Dolton parents weren't accepting of such possibilities.

Every day after school we played football, baseball or basketball at Kandy Kane. In the winter the men from the park district would come to the park, hook up a fire hose to the corner hydrant, and flood the center of the park to create a beautiful ice rink. Once the ice froze, often as early as November, we raced home from school, threw down our metal lunch boxes, kicked off our school shoes, and flew out the door with our ice skates and hockey sticks. The same men from the Dolton Park District staff came around in June to all the parks and took the rims off the backboards to prevent the black kids from Chicago from coming around to play basketball. The rims came down each June and were placed back up in August when the summer ended. This was more than some routine action; it was endemic of the racism that permeated Dolton. But perhaps the most obvious examples of racism in Dolton were its two private lakes, the Piscateers Fishing Club and Izaak Walton League of America (aka "the Ikes").

Piscateers was a stone quarry which was later filled in as a lake for fishing, about a mile across in both directions and stocked with bass, bluegill, catfish, walleye and northern pike. For a while cops in Dolton were given honorary memberships to Piscateers. This perk ended, not coincidentally, around the same time Dolton hired its first female and black police officers in the 1980s.

The Izaak Walton Lake was on the other side of town, near the railroad yard, and was also originally a man-made quarry which filled with water when they accidentally hit a live spring while digging. Though the Izaak Walton League of American is a "swimming and fishing club" whose mission is to help conserve wildlife resources, its Dolton chapter was really more of a whites-only drinking club.

But it didn't occur to me as a kid that only white people were members of these two clubs. Piscateers' barb-wired fence and "PRIVATE" sign on the locked front gate suggested to others what those who were members already knew—members only, all others go away. Don't bother asking to join unless you are white and know someone who is already a member.

Since the only way to become a member of either the Ikes or Piscateers was to have two or three current members sponsor you, along with other restrictions such as having your application screened and approved by a board of directors, there was no chance non-whites could ever obtain memberships. This likely still stands true, making these two clubs a couple of white dots on an otherwise black page in Dolton.

We didn't spend much time at the Piscateers, given my Dad worked double and triple shifts all the time and women were not permitted to be there without their husbands. Neither club permitted women to obtain full memberships, a prohibition that has since been relaxed likely because memberships plummeted in the 1990s when all the white families fled the area.

So Dolton represents the primary metaphor for this book…it embodies memories of tremendous fun, teen-aged mischief, and the racism that consumed our lives. But it was more than just latent racism. We were part of a subconscious cultural ideology that controlled the thoughts and actions of an entire community. It was the effect of learned behavior becoming innate, just as wars over religions are fought for centuries without a truce called to examine the root of the disagreement; an inbred mistrust that plagued a generation of people and created an epidemic of intolerance, passed from parents to their kids, and then on to their kids' kids. We learned writing, arithmetic and reading in school each day, and after school we got a daily lesson in hate.

"Your football coach Mr. Gomez is coming to drop off your uniform, Billy. I hope he doesn't stay long. Mexicans sure smell up the house," my friend's mom said to Billy while we played catch with the football on his front lawn. Shortly after, Coach Gomez arrived and Billy's mom came out of the house onto the front porch to greet him, mostly to try to avoid having to invite him inside.

"Oh good morning, Coach! How wonderful to see you. Thanks so much for dropping this off, see you at practice. Say hi to your wife for me!" She grabbed the uniform and hurried back in, leaving Mr. Gomez awkwardly standing on the porch alone.

While hanging out at my friend Jay's house, an old black man pulled up to drop off Jay's dad's car after being serviced.

"Hey fellas. Is your dad home?"

"Yes," Jay replied, "just go to the side door."

Before nearing the door Jay's mom came out and said, "Holy shit, even the niggers are coming around these days. Quick, let the Doberman out before something gets stolen!" The man just smiled and nervously laughed.

These examples were typical of the attitudes and beliefs Dolton residents held toward people of color. In fact, uttering support for people of color or gays would be perceived as highly abnormal back then. Growing up, I never met a single adult who didn't utter some racial epithet, instilling in my friends and me at a very young and impressionable age mistrust if not hatred toward anyone and everyone who didn't look white. The stereotypes passed through my ears and influenced my mind. They entered my subconscious and indelibly etched themselves on the blackboard of my brain. Whites were better than blacks. Blacks weren't to be trusted. All the adults said so, so we accepted the words as truth. After all, how could our parents be wrong? But I balanced this with my initial recollection of who the Dolton heroes were—the black basketball stars from Thornridge that the entire community rallied around and cheered for. How could I reconcile such a love-hate relationship?

We played Pop Warner football at Dolton Park, and although there were only a few black kids on the team at the time, they were among the better players. Certainly the fastest. My friend's dad told us this was because, "Their bodies are made differently. Blacks are built to run, but for some reason they just can't ice skate."

As a white kid who played lots of little league sports, the first time I saw true athletic talent was when I met a little black kid named Tyrese Bryant. What an athlete. The first season he played pee wee football he scored a touchdown about every time he touched the ball. In fact, Coach Gomez ran the same play to start every game—sweep right power shift. The other teams knew the play was coming. It didn't matter. They didn't have anyone fast enough to catch Tyrese. Same for basketball. We played together on the Lincoln Eagles Middle School team and finished the season 23-0 in 1981 behind Tyrese at point guard. Tyrese was a natural born athlete with incredible potential, heir apparent to Quinn Buckner.

Then at Thornridge High, Tyrese lost it all. Hung out with gang-bangers from nearby Harvey and Phoenix, got into drugs and alcohol, and pissed it all away. He was playing with his friend's dad's pistol one night and shot himself in the arm, then initially tried to tell police it was a van full of white kids who shot at him and his friends during a drive-by. In the biggest high school game of his career, when the college scouts came to see him, he fumbled the ball three times, costing us the game and him any chance of getting to college.

Growing up and competing in sports with black kids, at least to my white friends and me, was no big deal. I didn't experience for myself all the negative things my parents and other parents warned us of. "Don't trust them." "Don't let them get the upper hand." "Don't let the black boys talk to the white girls." There were differences in dress and dialect, but in general, Hispanic kids and black kids were pretty much the same as white kids—liked to have fun and didn't take school too seriously. Their actions, their words, and their hopes and dreams didn't align with how our parents characterized them. But most kids swallowed whole the rations of hatred their parents fed them, so racial tensions existed and plenty of white kids mistrusted black kids, and vice versa.

When a cross was burned on the lawn and a brick thrown through the front picture window of the first black family that moved into my neighborhood, my eyes were opened to what hate really looks like. Not just hateful feelings and words that I was already accustomed to hearing as a kid, but venomous, painfully hateful actions. When I rode my bike by the house and saw the kids picking up the broken glass, a little black boy still holding the brick that flew into his living room, I was consumed with guilt. I didn't know who committed the act, but I felt just as responsible. I saw tears in the eyes of the family members, and connected with them in a way that changed me forever. Why were these people not welcome to live here? Why was skin color a determining factor in whether they should be accepted or not? As I rode my bike back home after making eye contact with the mother sweeping glass off her porch, I began to cry. And it occurred to me then that wet tears streaming down a white cheek look the same as those streaming down a black one.

By the late 1970s the dream for white families in Dolton ended, interrupted by the same dream for black families leaving Chicago's troubled neighborhoods and housing projects in search of a better life. Our parents left Chicago in the 1950s and 1960s for a suburban experience devoid of diversity, and when black families left Chicago in the 1970s and 1980s for a better life, white families fled once again. Thousands of black families poured out of Chicago's poor neighborhoods seeking suburbs such as Dolton as a move up. The landscape of the south suburbs of Chicago changed overnight, and white families put their homes on the market and fled to other predominantly white Chicago suburbs or northwest Indiana. Dolton was, for the longest time, a mostly white suburb. When I was a kid it was over 90% white. Today it is over 90% black.

With our parents scattering like mice running for higher ground during a flood, there was no chance for my friends and me to maintain ties and later raise our own families together in the community we grew up in. Our parents called it "block busting," which they accused real estate agents of using as a strategy to entice whites to sell their homes to minorities. No enticement was necessary actually. White families were so afraid to live next to someone of color that as soon as an African-American, Hispanic, Asian, or Indian family moved on the block, ten For Sale signs went up within days. The exodus of white people from the south suburbs in the 1980s erupted with great force, and significantly altered the demographics of the Chicago region. Most whites wouldn't even try to cohabitate with anyone other than whites. Everyone went in different directions, and there was no Internet to keep us connected. There was no tolerance for an integrated community experience in a small suburb, and racism's hold strangled any hope for blacks and whites to cohabitate. It was only when I got to college that I saw the situation for what it really was—a generation of uneducated Baby Boomer parents whose own parents instilled in them a powerful xenophobic ideology, and who naturally passed the same sentiments directly to their kids.

When you're growing up in the suburb of a major city, the city is at first just one big mystery, like Oz behind the curtain. You hear everyone talking about it, you see its images on television and in the newspaper, and you feel the buzz about its sports teams. My parents didn't like the traffic and congestion of the city, so we didn't go there much as a family. As a little kid I knew of a place called Chicago and that it wasn't far from Dolton, I just had no idea what it looked like. Then I went there for the first time, and its wonderment was revealed.

When I was seven I took the CTA train downtown for a doctor's appointment with my Mom. Chicagoland is etched with miles and miles of train tracks, cutting through nearly every suburb where residents patiently turn off their car engines at railroad crossings while what seems like a million boxcars slowly roll by. In later years I took the Amtrak to WIU, spending most of the trip in the bar car drinking draft beer with other college students making their way to Illinois State, U of I, SIU and Eastern. But better than rides on the CTA and Metra were the rides on the Chicago "L." The L stands for "elevated train," because it is mostly above ground clickety-clacking over Chicago's streets and within inches of its various buildings. It was built in 1892, and when you ride it you are reminded of this fact, given how unstable it feels. But it remains the primary conveyance for over 700,000 people to and from work each day.

On the CTA with Mom, the city's enormity was awesome as we grew closer. Mom was in the middle of a long story about Mrs. O'Leary's cow kicking over a lantern in her barn, which started the Great Chicago Fire in 1871. But I wasn't paying attention. The CTA rolled toward Chicago through the middle of the Dan Ryan Expressway, the buildings in the distance becoming larger and larger, rearing up in front of me like a tall man slowly getting out of bed in the morning. Only through a little kid's eyes it was a family of tall men standing side by side, huddled close together in different shapes, sizes, and colors. The Sears Tower, the Hancock Building, Standard Oil. My Mom pointed each skyscraper out as we got closer.

After the doctor's appointment we explored the city streets and stopped for lunch at Gino's Pizza. Mom said it was the best pizza on the planet, and kidded me that Al Capone used to eat there. She was right about the pizza though, and I was stuffed after only one slice (years later I argued with her that Pizzeria Uno's and Aurelio's were actually better; it's an on-going debate). And the only thing more impressionable about that first visit to the city than its size and lunch were the people we passed on the city streets.

Chicago was my first exposure to black people, yellow people, brown people, and people of various shapes and sizes. A veteran with one leg in a wheelchair wearing a camouflage jacket with an American flag on his shoulder, begging for change. Asians, Mexicans, Orthodox Jews wearing kippahs. Scantily clad women cruising the street corners of the red light district near Rush Street. Street musicians banging drums and blowing horns as passersby dropped money into their buckets. I asked Mom a million questions that day, and she tried to help me put it all into perspective. She told me the funny looking guy with pale skin and white hair was called an "albino." Dolton didn't have any that I was aware of, but seeing one for the first time was intriguing.

The trips to the city increased with frequency as we became teenagers, especially after we got cars. Driving meant freedom, and freedom meant exploration. Like other large American cities, Chicago was the beating pulse of the region, its highways and roads connecting to it like arteries and veins to a heart pumping and beating 24/7. The highways revived us from the gradually suffocating town which by our teenage years we knew front and back. I learned the highways leading to the city just as I had learned the streets of the suburbs. It was along the Dan Ryan and Calumet Expressways where people made their way to and from work, and where visitors from all over the U.S. came to see the great City of Chicago.

Along these same highways for two summers in college, I worked for the Illinois Department of Transportation (IDOT) picking up trash along the road among its sea of billboards. IDOT was a strange place to work, where the luck of the draw dictated which crazy driver you were assigned to ride with each day, none of whom were terribly interested in actually doing any legitimate work. Most days we just parked the large orange IDOT trucks under a shady roadside tree or under an overpass, napping with eyes closed behind dark sunglasses. Other days we snuck off to local pubs for liquid lunches, or drank beer from brown paper sacks right in the trucks. One driver spent his days picking up stray hubcaps off the road, only to deliver them at the end of the day to his garage on the south side to sell. Another spent the day making buys from his local drug connection, rolling joints in the cab of the truck as I thumbed through the sports section of the *Chicago Tribune*.

But when I was twelve I started babysitting for neighbors' kids, and my neighbor John said instead of paying me he would take me to see a Bears game. As we entered Soldier Field I was awestruck by the enormity of the stadium and its beautiful green grass. I was fixated on number 34's every move. Was I really in the same stadium as Walter Payton, the hero I watched on television every Sunday? Later trips to Comisky Park for White Sox games and to Chicago Stadium for Blackhawks and Bulls games revealed the best thing about living near a major city. Chicago has arguably the best sports teams and most devoted fans in the country. And when the old Chicago Stadium wasn't being used for Bulls and Blackhawks games, it was used to expose a million Illinois and Indiana kids to the sheer joy of rock music.

Can anyone really forget the first rock concert they attended? I was only ten years old. It was March 30, 1977. Sammy Hagar opened for Boston at Chicago Stadium. Tony Jurgeto and I sat in little metal folding chairs 20 rows from the stage. An era where there were no special effects, no laser light shows, and no elaborate video displays. Only pure unadulterated rock and roll. Bias aside, I

11

would argue that the 1970s and 1980s were the best era of rock music. Our Baby Boomer parents and their radio stations acclimated our Generation X ears to rock in the late 1960s, feeding our eventual hunger for the harder rock of the 1970s and 80s—just as the original rock era of the 1950s piqued our parents' taste for the Beatles and Monkees in the 1960s.

Kids from 200 suburbs used Chicago as their gateway to the rock gods of the era—Zeppelin, Skynyrd, UFO, REO, Styx, Journey, Scorpions, RUSH, the Cars, The Police, Boston, AC/DC, Judas Priest...These mystical icons triggered in my generation a mutual cultural connection that provided us our own language and perspective. The music pulled us through meaningless school lectures, helped us cope with peer pressure, played in the background as we groped each other in back seats, and galvanized us at basement keg parties. Older brothers and sisters turned us on to what they were listening to, and hooked us to the pulsing drum beats and incendiary guitar riffs that have since been obliterated and watered down by other genres of music.

We were educated on the streets of Dolton, but Chicago was our playground, our recess. Each trip to the city was a mini-adventure, and I treasured each one and tucked it away in the Dewey Decimal System of my brain so I could pull them out later in life, revisiting each journey again for the first time. The visits to Chicago are still vivid in my memory—my grandmother taking my brothers and me to see the holiday window decorations at Macy's, then ice skating at Water Tower Plaza. Taste of Chicago on Navy Pier. Marching in the St. Patty's Day Parade along the green Chicago River with the Thornridge Marching Band, and dropping my drum stick just as the WGN television camera turned to focus on me. Redemption two years later when I got to play with the WIU drum line during the halftime show at a Bears game at Soldier Field.

Every kid from Dolton had similar experiences with the city, their city. And each one believed they could score like Tom Cruise in Risky Business, or play hooky from school like Ferris Bueller. With every trip we took into the city, my friends and I discovered something new. China Town, Greek Town, Jew Town, Wrigleyville, Little Italy...each neighborhood had a nickname correlating with its people and what it stood for. Chicago has always been one of the most ethnically diverse cities in the United States, where Greek,

Italian, Hispanic, African-American and Polish families maintained residence in diverse neighborhoods dating back to when their ancestors arrived in the United States.

But I can't talk about Chicago without a brief digression about politics. It's the city where Richard J. Dailey's "machine" ran for 21 years from 1955-1976. Dailey, aka "the boss," not only ran Chicago, he *was* Chicago. Dailey would have likely been elected to serve many more years had he not died in office, leaving behind him a history of autocratic city management and the famous quote, "The police are not here to create disorder, they're here to preserve disorder."

Daily was followed later by the first and only female mayor of Chicago, Jane Byrne, from 1979-1983. Byrne hired the city's first black superintendent, worked to recognize Chicago's gay residents, and briefly moved into Chicago's dangerous Cabrini Green housing complex alongside notorious Gangster Disciple gang-bangers, in order to bring attention to the plight of Chicago's poor and dangerous housing projects. Byrne was followed by the first black mayor in Chicago history, Harold Washington, who also died in office. Then from 1989-2011 Dailey's son Richard Jr. held the office for the longest term ever. Chicago politicians often kept pace with the ignominious reputation of Illinois politicians, including four governors (Kerner, Walker, Ryan, and Blagojevich) who were convicted of crimes.

As kids we weren't interested in politics or current news, but our parents were. They watched the nightly Chicago news channels where most of the focus was on the city itself, not its surrounding suburbs. The 'burbs were ancillary to the mother ship, floating behind it and riding in its current mostly as an afterthought. In the wake of it all we went about our business as kids, mostly listening in on parent conversations about the news of the day, but not really understanding its significance. Teachers attempted to illuminate the meaning of what was happening in the city: race relations, teacher strikes, crime and poverty. But these weighty issues held no significance for us. I never thought too long and hard about real issues until I was in college. Everything that preceded college was recess.

Dolton had no large buildings, so you could see brilliant stars on clear summer nights. But as we made our way toward Chicago,

13

the bright lights of the city consumed more stars the closer we got, eventually absorbing all of them in the glow that reflected from the city onto the hovering sky above. The same stars reappeared as the city's skyscrapers got smaller as we made our way home after each excursion.

We connected with the Windy City and understood what it was about more and more each visit, and it placed us in a trance that pulled us back with stronger force as we became less dependent on our parents and tired of the offerings of the little suburbs. The cacophonous echo of traffic resonating off skyscrapers as we walked the Magnificent Mile; holding on to the profusely shaking steel girders supporting the L tracks overhead; the deafening thunder of 50,000 Bears fans deliriously celebrating another touchdown, jumping and hugging complete strangers standing in sub-arctic temperatures; the first field trip to the Brookfield Zoo or Shedd Aquarium; the smell of dead fish washed up along Oak Street Beach. Chicago spoke to our senses, and captured our hearts.

Growing up in a small suburb, I realized there was a great big world beyond its borders. Through its liberation, the city gave me hope, and year by year my eyes opened wider to the bigotry that my little town embraced. But Dolton was my hometown. It was what I knew and was of the people that mattered to me. It profoundly affected and left an indelible mark on me. Over time I struggled to balance my sense of small town pride with the shame I felt for our attitudes. This created turmoil in my heart and mind, and reconciling this imbalance was most difficult. Even for all its shortcomings Dolton embraced us, and we embraced it back—clinging to it much like even a battered child hugs an abusive parent. It gave my friends and me the roots from which boys grow to become sturdy men. And as we grew the roots grew stronger, binding us beneath the soil and making it harder to emerge and break free. And when we finally did, we were transplanted to scattered places, leaving us the chance for reflection, reconnection, and redemption.

MORGAN, THE GREEN MONSTER AND THE ORGANIZATION

Scott from my baseball team approached me at practice one day and said, "This guy Jim I go to school with plays guitar and wants to start a band. I told him you play drums, and he said to give him a call."

The following weekend Jim Morgan came over with his guitar and we plugged it into my dad's reel-to-reel player. He proceeded to play the riff from Freebird and a few bars of Purple Haze, and we jammed for two hours straight. My first rock band Sinjiin (pronounced "sin-gin") was born. One of four kids from a stable, upper-middle crust household, "Morgs" was a great guitar player at only age 12. We both lived in Dolton, but on separate school boundary lines, so we attended different elementary and middle schools.

Morgan was a bit of a tech nerd, but in a way everyone respected because they knew he was going to be very successful someday. He was thin-framed and wiry, the perfect build for a gymnast, which he also excelled in. Brown hair parted down the middle, and the makings of a promising moustache already. He graduated from high school a year early, earned a Bachelor's Degree in electrical engineering from Purdue, and then an MBA from Duke. If I ever made it to *Who Wants to be a Millionaire*, Jim would be my "phone-a-friend." He approaches life a step ahead of everyone else, and understands that the most successful people in life play chess, not checkers.

At 38 he started his own communications consulting firm. Jim can fix virtually anything that is broken, and has a penchant for breaking or taking things apart just to see if he can put them back together. We still jam whenever we're together, but after he left for college the realization that we were not going to be the next KISS set in. I think it set in much earlier than that for him, but he never let on that we had no chance for careers in music. I was more naïve and, as a result, much more disappointed when Sinjiin broke up after high school. Most of our youth was spent practicing music, playing sports, and getting into trouble. And a good amount of this trouble centered on "The Green Monster."

Growing up, we were a one-car (technically a one-van) family. In order to cart four boys to and from football and baseball practices, boy scout meetings, and other weekend activities, my parents purchased a used Ford Econoline van. This thing was about the size of a gutted out ice cream truck, only uglier. Ours was two shades of green accented with a trim of rust along the bottom. My friends thought the Walker van, also known as The Green Monster, was totally cool (probably because we could pack lots of girls and beer in it). Little did I know when my parents purchased it how useful the Monster would be in a pinch.

By eighth grade the following year we found two other fledgling musicians to jam with, and had developed a list of four songs we could play from start to finish. My parents never complained, but I'm sure hearing over and over Judas Priest's "Living After Midnight" and "Breaking The Law," with AC/DC's "Back in Black" and Black Sabbath's "Paranoid" was nothing short of sheer torture for them. One January night we were finishing band practice in my basement. Morgan was particularly quiet that night, and I could tell something was on his mind. After the other guys packed up and left, Morgan and I stood out on my front curb as he waited for his dad to pick him up. I figured I would use the time to find out what was on his mind.

"Dude, are you pregnant or something? You're like a total space cadet tonight. What's the deal?"

Morgan set his guitar down and said in a serious tone, "The Organization is coming after me. I'm really shitting my pants, and I can't tell my parents. I need your help. Come by my house tomorrow after school and I'll show you the letter."

At Dirksen Junior High, Morgan's school, there was a secret club known as The Organization which attempted to terrify other kids. Jim had heard about The Organization, and his older brother Tommy teased him to watch out for it as he was heading into Dirksen. But Jim assumed the club was more myth than reality. It wasn't unusual for members to crank call other kids, play ding-dong dash on them, or send them hate mail which usually consisted of words spelled out with letters cut and pasted from the newspaper. But he never thought The Organization would target him. He never thought they would actually harm anyone.

After school the next day, I hopped on my ten-speed and made my way toward Morgan's house three miles away. The whole anonymous letter thing was mysterious and exhilarating, so I made it to his house in record time. I arrived, hopped off my bike, and ascended the stairs up to his bedroom in four leaps. Morgan turned down the Jimi Hendrix album he was playing before presenting the letter to me.

"Check this out," he said, showing me the latest letter.

Sure enough, it was a strangely scripted page using cut out letters of all shapes and colors from the newspaper which read: "lEAve a $10 BILL in FrOnT OF loCKER 64 in D hALL monDAY MoRnING and DO noT TELL anYONe OR U dIE! thE OrgAnIZaTioN"

I laughed. "Whatever. What a bunch of losers."

Morgan was less assured, pacing his room and saying, "Yeah, but I don't want to get beat up, and I don't have $10 to spare." This wasn't actually true, since I knew full well he had been helping his dad fix radios and televisions in their make-shift basement shop since he was in fifth grade, and that his dad gave him some of the money they were paid for the repairs, which he usually spent on stuff for his guitar and amp. Later, when he was in high school, he made most of his money making fake IDs for underage kids who wanted to buy beer.

"Do you know any members of this little boy scout troop?" I asked in an attempt to calm him down, trying to make him laugh.

But he replied in a serious tone, "Not really. I know the two kids who pushed me off my bike last weekend, and I think they are part of The Organization. They live a few blocks from here. Mike, what the fuck am I going to do?"

"Are your parents going out again this weekend?"

Morgan thought for a second and then it occurred to him, "Yeah. They have some party at St. Jude's Saturday night."

"Okay. Didn't you say you've been sneaking their car out lately when they're gone? Can you get wheels that night?"

"My dad usually takes the Cutlass and leaves the Wagoneer here, so if my brother and sisters are out I can get the spare keys."

"Okay. You focus on getting the truck for Saturday night, and leave the rest to me. We're going to send a little message to this so-called 'Organization.'"

Morgan had two older sisters and an older brother, and it was a tradition in his family for the kids to sneak their parents' cars out at very young ages, and each Morgan kid had driving-related incidents. According to Morgan, his oldest sister Deb snuck the car out when she was 14. His sister Lori had that beat by a year, taking it out at 13, though when she failed to use the brake when returning the car to the garage one night and took out the back wall, this put Jim's brother Tom at a distinct disadvantage. Tommy let his buddy Larry Kane drive Mr. Morgan's car, they had an accident, and Tom covered for Kane. After these disasters, his dad started checking the mileage before and after going out at night. As a result, Tommy didn't get to sneak the car out much before he got his license. But later, Tommy took Jim and me along with his college buddies to the Indy 500, where we got drunk all weekend, slept in tents and got to see topless girls. So Tommy was my earliest hero and a legend in our eyes.

There were six years between Jim and Tommy, so by the time his brother and sisters were in college and out of the house, his dad had relaxed on his suspicions about the car. Other than Morgan getting pinched for using his dad's corporate calling card for ringing up $1,400 in long distance calls after he began dating a girl named Rita we met at a campsite in Indiana, he was on pretty good footing with his parents. Actually, Morgan was way more deviant than his siblings, he was just much better at concealing his mischief than they were.

So Saturday night came and Morgan and I hung out at his house practicing our music as his parents got ready to head for their big night out at St. Jude's Church, only a few blocks from their house. His dad yelled up from the kitchen as they departed, "Jim, we're leaving. We're taking The Wagon because it's starting to snow. See you later tonight."

"Shit," Morgan whispered. "We're screwed. There are no spare keys for the Cutlass, only The Wagon. And the Cutlass can't handle the snow."

"O.k. dad. Have fun!" Morgan yelled down as the back door closed.

18

"So what. We just walk to Jude's and take it from there, then return it after we're done," I said.

"Man, that's risky. What if they leave early and notice it's gone? They'll think it got stolen and call the cops."

"Of all the times I've crashed here and your parents have been out, they never made it home before midnight. It's only seven now, and we can have it back before ten no prob."

Morgan wasn't wild about the idea, but he knew I would call him a sissy if he didn't go along, so he shook his head in agreement. "My dad's a cop, so even if we get pinched we'll just say we were goofing around. Plus, this way you won't chance driving the old man's Cutlass through the back of your garage like Lori did," I jabbed.

"Actually, that was nothing compared to when Deb was a freshman at Western and she and her friends were cracking beers on the way back to campus and she missed a turn and drove her car through a corn field. Tore the entire undercarriage out. Let's go sneak a few beers before we head over. I need a buzz before we pull this off."

I could see by now Jim was totally excited about the night ahead, and before we finished our last song he did a Pete Townsend 360 strum on his electric guitar then stuck out his tongue and gave me the "long live rock and roll" sign with his right hand (arm extended high above his head, hand closed except the thumb, index finger and pinky).

Morgan's family had an extra refrigerator in their detached garage, usually full of beer and wine, so he ran to grab a few Old Styles. His dad drank Old Style, mine drank Strohs, and back then we thought these were top shelf beers. Only years later did we realize what swill we were drinking as kids. I looked out the kitchen window to see Morgan emerge from the garage with four cans of beer clutched against his chest, arms folded like King Tut. But he attempted to do a running slide back toward the house, and slipped on his ass and the beers flew everywhere, shooting through the snow like meteors.

"Nice job, ace," I remarked as I walked out back to help him dig the beers out of the snow.

We sat at the kitchen table and played a few games of quarters. His Formica table was the best for bouncing quarters into a cup of beer, which was the drinking game of choice when we were kids. Later in high school while playing a game of speed quarters at a party, Morgan swallowed the quarter. Every day in school for the next few weeks kids came up to Jim and asked, "Excuse me, do you have any extra change on, I mean *in* you I can borrow?" We finished our beers and Morgan grabbed the spare keys to The Wagon (as Morgan's family referred to their Jeep Wagoneer truck) from his dad's underwear drawer and we got bundled up to head out. As we left his house I couldn't help wonder whether his dad hid the spare truck keys under his skivvies out of convenience, because he believed it an unlikely place his kids would look, or perhaps to dissuade them from reaching in to find them.

The falling snow blanketed the ground, which was already covered with a few inches of snow from recent snowfall. The flakes were thick and wet, so the packing was great. We pelted each other with snowballs during the walk to the church, ducking behind parked cars parked along the street for cover. It was near nine o'clock when we arrived, and by now the event in the community center next to the church had started. A few more people hustled inside, but mostly the lot was empty. It didn't take long for us to locate The Wagon. Though it was snowing, the moon was incredibly full and bright, its face looking directly down at Morgan and me as if preparing to judge us for our upcoming indiscretions. I stood staring up at it, caught in a moment of wonderment. It reminded me of a part in the book I was currently reading for my literature class: Fitzgerald's *The Great Gatsby*, and the symbolism of the morality of man viewed through the spectacled eyes on the billboard of Dr. T.J. Eckleburg. I wasn't much for school, but I liked reading stories with lots of hidden meanings.

We hopped into The Wagon and surveyed the lot to make sure no one was looking. At thirteen as an eighth grader Morgan didn't pass for much older than fifteen, still under the legal driving age of sixteen. Morgan started the truck and put it in gear like he had been performing these functions for years. We pulled out of the lot and even with the windows closed I could hear the crunch of the snow under the tires. I had mostly only been in cars my parents had driven, but Morgan looked really natural behind the wheel.

"Dude, be really careful. Your dad will kill you if you crack up his truck. You're the only hope he has left for raising a kid who hasn't done something really stupid with a car yet."

"No sweat. This baby has four wheel drive." I didn't know what that meant, but he stated it with enough confidence that I felt a little better about taking the truck out in bad weather. I just replied as though I knew what the hell he was talking about, "Cool. Perfect for a night like this."

We rounded the corner and headed a few blocks down the side streets with rows of identical houses. Some of the homes, like mine, had funky doorknobs in the middle of the front door instead of near the door frame. And most didn't have mailboxes at the curb. Instead, they had mail slots cut into the front of the house next to the door where the mailman dropped the envelopes, which landed on the floor of a small coat closet inside. This was ideal for climates such as Chicago's. No one would have wanted to walk to the curb for their mail during the winter months.

"Jason Streetmeyer lives a few houses up on the left. He's the one that pushed me off my bike last weekend. Right into the shrubs. Messed me up pretty bad. I think he's the one who sent the letter," Morgan frowned.

"Okay. Park the truck a few houses up, but leave the motor running," I said. He pulled over, turned the lights off, and left the car running. Now the snow was coming down really hard and fast, making visibility difficult. We got out and crept toward Jason's house.

Jim whispered to me, "Give me the M-80 and the lighter. I'll light it and drop it on the front porch just as you ring the bell," he instructed.

"Man, this is going to be awesome." I grinned with excitement.

An M-80 is a large firecracker packed with gunpowder, the equivalent of several packs of regular firecrackers, and would most definitely scare the heck out of anyone inside a house if it were detonated on their porch. We didn't see many lights on inside, but we hadn't really thought much about what would happen after we lit the wick and dropped the Pez dispenser-sized explosive onto the porch at the base of the door. But as we approached the house, Jim caught sight of the mail slot next to the front door. Suddenly he had a different plan in mind.

21

As he lit the wick and dropped the M-80 into Jason's mail slot, and before I could ring the doorbell, the front porch light came on and the door flew open. We ran off the porch toward the running Wagon and heard someone yell, "We got you now! Get back here! We're gonna kick your—" I didn't hear the rest of the sentence, as it was drowned out by an enormous explosion that echoed as the M-80 exploded inside the house. The sound rang out through the surrounding neighborhood, reverberating through the cold night air enough to make my ears ring as we jumped into The Wagon and peeled away. In the rearview mirror I could see three guys running out of the house and into a car parked across the street.

"Dude! Turn your lights on before you hit something!" I yelled.

"I don't want them to see us. Damn, Jason's older brother must have been home!"

"His older brother? You didn't say anything about an older brother!" I could see they had already started their car and were pursuing us, their headlights getting larger in our review as they closed in. "Holy shit. We're freakin' dead meat. What do we do? Should we drive back to St. Jude's?"

"Right. Let's peel into a church parking lot in a truck I'm not supposed to be driving and tell my dad we need his protection from three guys chasing us because we dropped a small bomb into their house. Good plan, peanut head." Morgan emphasized his frustration by taking his hands off the wheel and gesturing toward me.

"Shit! Get your hands on the wheel!" I yelled, as the car veered all over the road. I reached for my seatbelt and put it on. Morgan did the same.

"Okay. Head toward my house. With any luck Dave is home and we can get inside before they catch us. At least then it will be a fair fight," I said, checking the rearview again to gauge their distance behind us. They were fish tailing all over the road too, so we were able to maintain our distance.

"Man, I forgot to engage the four wheel drive," Morgan said as he reached for the console between the front seats and pulled on a lever. Suddenly The Wagon stopped swerving and the ride felt much more stable. Morgan hit the gas and the truck began to separate from our pursuers. He was handling the road well under the snowy conditions, and the wiper blades kept time with Baba O-Rily blaring on the radio, cutting a clear viewpoint through the heavy snow pelting the windshield.

As exhilarating as the chase was, I kept picturing Jim and me standing in front of our parents explaining how we stole the Morgans' truck, drove without a license, blew up someone's mail slot, and crashed in a high speed chase. Even being the son of a cop wasn't going to get me out of such a mess. But I shifted my focus to the chase in order to help Morgan avert our pursuers and try to get out of this alive. With the crappy weather there weren't many cars on the road, and we turned onto Sibley Boulevard. We were getting closer to my neighborhood.

"Take a left at the next light at Greenwood. You should be able to punch it on the straight away and get ahead of them," I said to Jim, who was totally focused on his driving and seemed deep in thought, as though he was engineering some magical solution to our not-so-minor dilemma.

"I'm not going to have to punch it. I'm going to time my turn on yellow just before the light turns red, and they'll be stuck at the light."

I wasn't sure what that meant, but it seemed Jim had a plan so that was all that mattered. All I cared about was losing them.

Morgan relaxed on the accelerator about a block before the intersection, and we could see the light was still green as we approached. But in doing so, their car gained considerable ground on ours. As we rolled toward the light, green turned to yellow. By now they were right behind us. But instead of coming to a complete stop, as the light turned from yellow to red, Jim floored it and blazed through the intersection, just missing two cars that had the right of way. As he turned onto Greenwood, I looked back to see Jason's car stuck at the intersection. Morgan hit the accelerator and turned down the first side street, now slowing down so as not to attract attention.

"Shit! That was awesome. Dude, you're fucking Mario Andretti! Unbelievable!" I grabbed Jim and shook him, unable to control my enthusiasm in the moment. Jim smiled proudly and replied, "That's right. I *am* Mario Andretti. Next stop, Indy!"

As we approached Kandy Kane Park near my house, Morgan decided—much to my surprise—to celebrate our narrow escape with a little night drive through the park. Without notice he turned off the headlights, cranked the wheel and the car hopped the snow-covered curb. He reached over and flipped the lever to turn off the four wheel drive. Much like the carnival rides we enjoyed every summer, Morgan was now speeding through the park and swerving left and right to fishtail the back of the car. In the middle of the park he attempted to do a 360, when suddenly the car stopped and the wheels just kept spinning in the snow.

"What happened?" I asked, turning my head toward Jim as he pumped the accelerator with his foot.

"Shit. I think we're stuck."

"Stuck? How can we be stuck? You're one block from my house and Jason and his crew may come this way any minute. Besides, what the hell happened to four wheel drive, Mr. Andretti?!"

Sensing my frustration, Morgan dropped the gears from forward to reverse to try to rock it out of the rut we were in. Smoke rose from the whirring tires and I smelled rubber burning. He was only digging in deeper. He tried engaging the four wheel drive, but this too failed given the truck was not in motion. He turned off the engine and hopped out. I followed him, slamming the door harder than I intended.

"Dude, if those guys know what direction we were heading, we're dead meat!" I reminded him.

"I doubt they know you were with me," he reassured, "you don't even go to my school. But we're going to need a shovel. Can we walk to your house from here to get one?"

"Just leave The Wagon in the middle of the park?"

"Do you have a better plan?"

I looked at my watch and it was nearly ten o'clock. I remembered that my Dad was working midnights tonight, meaning he would be leaving for work around now to begin his shift at the police station. This would also mean that my Mom would be going to sleep soon after seeing him off, and that a squad car would be picking him up at the house any minute now to drive him to work.

"Well we can walk there to get a shovel, but if my dad's ride drives by this way, we're definitely pinched."

We bailed on the truck and the park was quiet. The snowfall was tapering off, and only a few small flakes were gently falling from the black sky. Through the cold night air, only the echo of the boxcars connecting in the distant Riverdale rail yard was audible. As we walked up the alley nearing the back of my house the moon shone brightly, still surveying Jim and me like a shepherd watches his flock. I stopped, tilted my head back, and attempted to catch a snowflake on my tongue. The stars appeared close enough that I could reach up to play connect the dots, but my bemusement was interrupted by the honk of a car horn. I could see through the side yard that my Dad's ride had pulled up and was waiting for him in front of our house, the "Dolton Police" letters on the door and double cherry lights on the roof illuminated by the streetlight. We ducked behind two garbage cans to ensure we wouldn't be seen, and waited for the sound of the squad car to pull away. It was facing the opposite direction of the park. Our good fortune continued.

"Let me go in and see what the deal is. Wait here," I said.

The house was pitch dark and my youngest brother Dennis was already asleep. David and Todd were out for the night; my Mom's bedroom light was out and her TV was still on. The theme from MASH and several beers had lulled her to sleep as they usually did by this time each night, so I tiptoed toward her dresser, reached into her purse, and grabbed the keys to our van, The Green Monster.

I closed the back door quietly and made my way around the garage to the alley. "Where's the shovel?" Morgan asked.

"I got something better," I said as I jingled the keys in his face.

"Do you know how to drive?" he asked, well knowing the answer that would follow.

"No. But you do. It will take us all night to dig The Wagon out. We don't have that much time. Let's just push it out with The Green Monster."

The van was parked in the driveway next to our house, so we put it in neutral in order to push it out onto the street without needing to start the engine. After we rolled it into the road, we straightened the steering wheel and pushed it for a few houses until we were far enough from my house so that starting the engine wouldn't wake my Mom.

Morgan hopped in, started it up as expertly as he did The Wagon earlier, and we sped toward the park. As with The Wagon, he looked oddly at ease behind the wheel of my van. Not unlike how comfortable I've always felt behind a drum set, Morgan seemed one with a car. I think driving was somehow deeply embedded in his family genes. It came as natural to him as walking.

"Man. This thing rides high like a semi-truck or something," Morgan said, adjusting to the feel of the larger steering wheel and elevated height from the road. I could see him working it all out in his head.

"Just don't crash. I know it's a piece of shit, but it's the only piece of shit we own."

As we proceeded down Ellis Avenue toward the park a car pulled onto our road heading in our direction, its headlights resembling those we eluded earlier. Jim swiftly pulled over and turned off the headlights, and we ducked down waiting for the car to pass. As the car drove by we peeked up to see it was just a false alarm. Still no sign of Jason's car.

Morgan slipped the van into low gear as we approached the park, hopping the curb and making our way toward where The Wagon sat at rest in the dark, its rear tires halfway immersed in snow. He located the same tire tracks we made earlier, and slowly lined up the back of his truck with the front of The Green Monster. When he was about a foot away he stopped and put the van in park.

"Ok. Now all you need to do is get into my truck and start it up. Then put it in drive and wait for me to push you out. As you feel me pushing on your rear, hit the gas and we should be out no problem," he instructed. "The gas pedal is the one on the right."

"Got it. Just don't push on my rear too hard," I joked, making Jim take a playful swing at me as I hopped out of the van.

I got into his truck and started it up, put it in gear and held my foot over the gas while looking at Morgan through the review mirror. I heard and felt the van make contact with me, and the truck inched forward a bit. Just then I accelerated and could feel the rear wheels furiously spinning. A high pitched whizzing came from the wheels while smoke plumed from the tires. The Green Monster's engine roared, and I could feel The Wagon inching forward. With a simultaneous acceleration of both vehicles, The Wagon finally lunged forward and out of the rut, settling on flat snow a few feet ahead. But without looking back at Jim in the van, I abruptly hit the brake too soon. In an effort not to get the van stuck in the same rut, Morgan accelerated and plowed into the back of his truck with The Green Monster, smashing out the entire row of taillights on The Wagon. The Monster, steel bumper and all, was undamaged.

I looked back to see Morgan clasping his hands on the top of his head, and I could easily make out the only word he uttered: "FUCK!"

"What the hell did you stop for?" he yelled as he jumped from the van.

"You didn't tell me what to do next. You know I've never drove before! Man, I'm sorry, dude." I really was sorry, though at the same time was relieved the van was undamaged. While driving at an early age was common in the Morgan household, it would have sent my Mom and Dad over the edge for sure.

We stood there for a second, pondering our fate, still praying that our pursuers weren't heading our way. But that part of the night was now somehow a distant memory, and proportionately less important than what to do about the two vehicles in the middle of Kandy Kane Park. We thought for a second and then an idea came to mind.

"All we need to do is put the van back, then park the truck back at the church and drop the taillight pieces nearby so your dad will think it was a hit and run," I said, unsure such a half-baked plan would have any chance of working.

We turned the truck off, got back in the van and drove it toward my house. Three houses down we killed the headlights and engine, coasting like a stealth bomber quietly into our driveway. Jim earned his Andretti status right back, following precisely in the same tire tracks in the driveway we created when we pushed it out earlier. If the light snowfall continued overnight, the tracks would be completely covered. The Green Monster was right back where it started, having done its part to bail us out of the mess we were in. The face in the moon looked down with approval.

We ran back to the park and collected all the pieces of broken plastic taillights setting in the snow behind The Wagon, scooping up the red and clear pieces like confetti off a dance floor. We jumped in and drove out of the park. Once on the main roads, Morgan drove slowly. After all, my Dad was riding patrol at this very moment in a town about twenty square miles, and the likelihood of driving by him or a fellow officer was pretty good. Jason might still be out looking for us. We made it back to St. Jude's and most of the cars were still there, meaning the party was still going. My watch read 11:30.

"Do you remember which spot you pulled out of?" I asked.

"Definitely. I think it was that open one right there."

"Definitely is not *I think*. Are you sure or what?"

"I'm pretty sure. They'll be buzzed anyway. As long as it's close my dad probably won't notice."

We waited for a few other people to walk out of the side door of the community center next to the church, and then pulled into the spot. It did appear to be the same position we pulled The Wagon from earlier. I jumped out of the truck and began scattering the broken pieces of taillight below the rear of the truck. I paused to survey the back of Jim's father's car, and felt guilty that it was banged up. I was tempted to look up to the sky and check with the moon for reassurance, but was afraid he would be scowling down at me, making me feel worse than I already did. It looked as though someone with a hammer totally annihilated every light along the back, and the rear of the car reminded me of an angry jack-o-lantern. This would not be the image Morgan's old man would want to see after a night out. I tried not to picture the look on his and Jim's mom's faces as they approached the Wagon to head home. Jim was not as melancholy though.

"Damn drunk drivers leaving church functions. You just can't trust anyone these days!" Morgan said as he sprinkled tiny taillight pieces onto the ground like a farmer spreading chicken feed. He was finding much more humor in the situation than I. We locked the truck doors then hightailed it back to Morgan's house. He rushed to his parent's bedroom and put the keys back in his dad's not-so-secret hiding spot.

"Shit Morgs, what a night! If we pull all this off I'll be shocked. Shut your lights off until your dad gets home so Jason and his goons don't come around looking for you. Maybe he didn't know it was you, and he won't be looking to kill you Monday morning at school."

I picked up Jim's house phone and dialed the non-emergency number for the Dolton Police Department. "Hi. Can you ask Officer Walker to call his son at Jim Morgan's house? He knows the number. Thanks."

"My dad will call in a minute to come and pick me up and give me a ride home. If anything goes wrong on my end I'll call you tonight or first thing in the morning," I said.

Morgan reached into his dad's liquor cabinet, pulled the top off a bottle and took a swig, then grinned and handed me the bottle. "Here's to The Organization." I smiled and took a sip, making my face pucker.

"What the hell is Red Breast? Yuck!"

Just then the phone rang. Morgan answered it, and I could tell by his expression it wasn't my Dad calling to confirm my ride.

"Whoever it was hung up without saying anything," he said, though the look on his face suggested otherwise. He returned the phone to its cradle, and suddenly the phone rang again, this time making both of us jump. My heart began racing just as it did when we were escaping our pursuers earlier.

"Hey Mr. Walker…Sure, I will tell him you're on the way."

We waited in the living room at the front of the house to watch for my Dad's arrival, sitting on Morgan's sofa, which was covered in uncomfortable plastic wrap. The Red Breast warmed my chest and made me a little sleepy.

A few minutes passed, then my Dad pulled up in his squad car. Jim walked me to the front door, and as I descended his porch Jason's car passed slowly by the front of the house. But the timing was perfect. They didn't dare risk a confrontation with a cop car sitting there.

I woke the next morning to my Dad coming in after his shift. "Michael. Get your butt up and help your brothers shovel the snow," Dad yelled toward my room. I got dressed and made my way to the kitchen where my Dad was removing his holster as Mom handed him his morning coffee.

"I took a report at St. Jude's last night after I dropped you home. Someone backed into Jim's dad's car and left without leaving a note or anything," my Dad said somewhat matter-of-factly. He didn't sound suspicious.

"Man, that stinks," I said without making eye contact with him as I headed downstairs to dial Jim's number from the basement line. He answered before the second ring.

"Morgs, it's Mike. What's the deal on your end? My dad just came home and said he took a report for the damage at Jude's. I can't talk much now. He wants me outside helping to shovel the snow."

"Well good luck shoveling snow without your gloves. You left them on the front seat of my dad's truck."

EDDY AND JIMMY

They had little in common but everything in common. Eddy Hookman was my first best friend. The one against whom I measured and defined all friendships to follow. The type of friend I woke up and thought about first thing in the morning, and wanted to hang out with all day. Living only two doors down, this was easy. He was a huge part of my world from ages eight through thirteen. Jimmy Thoreau picked up where Eddy left off. He was one of my best friends throughout high school. We met when I tried out for the wrestling team, and hung out nearly every weekend.

Eddy and Jimmy are mostly connected in the little living room of the house that occupies my mind. Though they lived only two blocks from each other and were cordial, they weren't good friends. In the end they wound up together though. Eddy a kid with a dark, disruptive home life and no real motivation to do much with his future, and Jimmy with limited structure coming from a one-parent household where all the focus was on his athletic prowess as a wrestler. Not everyone who lived in Dolton got a chance to go to college. Those who made it out of Dolton got decent jobs in Chicago or in the nicer western and northern suburbs of the city. Those who couldn't afford college, which was most of my graduating class, took blue collar jobs in and around the south suburbs. Eddy and Jimmy did neither.

Eddy and I did everything together and spent most days after school playing pitch-catch, pretending to be big leaguers. The first thing I noticed when I met Eddy was that he had no fingernails. They were like little flakes of nail centered at the tip of each finger. After I got the courage to ask him about it, he said he lost his fingernails from accidentally slamming them in his mom's car door. I didn't think much of it at the time, but later understood his gnawed fingers to be the result of something entirely different. Nervously chewing on them as his mind raced about what could happen next in an uncertain and unstable home, an act that pacified him in bed at night as his stepfather's shadow passed before his bedroom doorway.

Eddy's family moved in two houses down from mine in June when I was eight, and I was excited to have someone my age in our neighborhood. He was a good looking kid, lean frame, long disheveled sandy brown hair hanging over his face, which masked bright blue eyes and freckles on his cheeks. There was Eddy who was seven; his sister Sandy, eleven; and his brother Sammy, eight. Sammy couldn't talk except to make strange sounds, and my Mom said he was retarded. At the time I didn't know what this meant, other than that he was different from the other kids on the block. Sammy could hear fine, he just couldn't speak, and his brain wasn't "properly developed," as Dad put it. He was the first kid I met who was different from all the other kids, and initially we made fun of him and called him "half-daff" (because he could hear but not speak, so we believed him to be only half retarded). But over time we took to him, and later defended him as one of our own. Eventually it was well known in our neighborhood not to mess with Sammy.

"Hey. My name is Mike. Want to play catch?" I asked Eddy the first day he came outside his house after moving in. Other than his gnarly fingernails and his brother who couldn't talk, Eddy seemed pretty cool. He smiled a lot and wasn't shy meeting new people. I was drawn to him from the first day we met. Eddy was full of life.

"I'm Ed. But everybody calls me Eddy. Sure. Only I can't find my mitt."

"I have an extra one, I'll get it," I ran to my garage, excited that I would have someone to throw the ball with other than Dad for a change.

I returned out front to find Eddy talking to his stepfather, Richard. My Mom had already given me the rundown on their family, so I knew Richard and Barbara recently married and that none of her three kids were Richard's. Sandy was from Barbara's first marriage, and Sammy and Eddy were from her second. Richard was her third husband.

"Edward, have you asked your mother or me if you can be outside playing? I suggest you get your behind inside and finish helping first," his stepdad said, hands on his hips looking sternly down at Eddy. While I had always called my father *Dad*, and he called me son, I quickly got used to the formality that Eddy and his stepfather held between them. Eddy was *Edward* to his stepfather, who would only be referred to by his family as Richard. Never father, and certainly never "dad."

"You must be one of the Walker boys. Edward will call you after he finishes his chores. Run along now," Richard said to me. I was disappointed that we wouldn't get to play catch that day, and it made me dislike Richard from the start. But this reason for disliking him paled in comparison to the reasons he would later give me for resenting him.

The next morning Eddy knocked at our front door and said he could play catch, so I grabbed both my gloves and headed out to the front yard. He seemed a bit down, so I asked him if anything was wrong.

"My mom and Richard had an argument last night, so he slept on the pull-out bed in the basement with our dog, So-So. It's really Richard's dog. Later on we couldn't find So-So, and then Richard opened the bed back up and found him inside, dead.

I was a bit freaked out by what Eddy just said, but it didn't seem to faze him too much.

"Come on, let's call signals for fastballs and curves. I'm left-handed, but I'll just wear the glove backwards," Eddy stated. I stared down at Eddy's hands, his chewed away fingernails, wondering what it must be like not to be able to throw with your right hand. This too seemed strange. I never met anyone who was left-handed, but it made Eddy all the more unique. Most things about Eddy were different than I was used to.

"Don't you have a baseball glove?" I asked.

"Oh, yeah, it's a Ted Williams Limited Edition. The best glove you can get. I just can't find it right now. We're still unpacking," Eddy said as he looked away and jumped off our front porch onto the lawn.

"Do you play on a team?" I asked.

"I played for like two years in Chicago, mostly pitcher, and then we moved here. But mom will sign me up for the team here right away."

"Cool. I played catcher this year, so you can pitch to me and I'll practice catching." After a few throws though, I realized Eddy wasn't very good, and I spent that first day shagging most of the balls he threw as they rolled down our Ellis Street. Old Mr. Glorioso sat on his front porch a few houses down, reading the newspaper and smoking his pipe, occasionally peering over the paper and shaking his head as I ran back and forth to retrieve Eddy's errant throws. The Chicago little league must not be very good, I thought, as I threw another misfired ball back to Eddy.

After we played catch we walked over to Eddy's house and hung out in his back yard. We talked about Eddy attending the same school as me in the fall, and being a year older than him told him which teachers to look out for. Our conversation was interrupted by Eddy's mom coming to the back door. This was the first time I had seen Eddy's mom up close. As her face came into focus through their screen door it appeared she had been crying and one of her cheeks was bright red, a cigarette loosely dangling from her lips.

"Edward, your dad and I are going to the store to pick up a few things. Please keep an eye on your brother while we're out. I don't know where Sandy has wandered off to," she said quietly and in a bit of a trance, and closed the door without acknowledging me standing right next to Eddy.

Over time I learned that having Eddy as a friend meant dealing with a series of lies. It wasn't that he was a bad kid. He just tried to fit in by stretching the truth. Later I realized that through telling lies Eddy was able to create a better existence than the one he lived. That was just how it was, and I didn't mind. At the time I figured he just had a wild imagination.

I remember some of Eddy's most common promises that he always talked about but which never came true: "My real dad is coming into town this weekend and is taking me shopping for new clothes…"

"We're getting a Doberman Pinscher, and I'm going to train him…"

"My mom is going to buy me a new Rawlings baseball glove and Louisville Slugger bat before baseball season…"

"Richard is going to let me drive the boat on Lake Michigan this weekend…"

But the day Eddy said, "Let's go to the carnival. My mom got paid and gave me twenty bucks to spend," I assumed he was telling the truth. After all, as we left his house on our bikes, his mom waved from the front porch and said, "Have a good time." Of all the fibs Eddy told, I remember this one clearest. And it was one he paid for dearest.

The Dolton Carnival was sponsored by the volunteer fire fighters' squad the first week of every July. We looked forward to it almost as much as Christmas. For four days and four nights around the Fourth of July, Dolton Park became a paradise for me and all the other kids in our neighborhood. The annual Dolton Parade kicked things off, and included dozens of fire engines, cop cars, floats, and frolicking clowns who threw us candy. Classic cars cruised by shining like new dimes. Motorcycles did figure eight moves and nearly crashed before our very eyes as they roared by. One year the Cub Scouts, who we always poked fun at, made a float and held a sign that read, "Hello Dolton," except the little kid holding the sign accidentally held his hand over the o in Hello. It didn't take much to make us snicker.

We would save up our money from mowing lawns all spring, then stuff ourselves on cotton candy, hot dogs, ice cream, and rides on the Tilt-o-Whirl, Ferris Wheel, or Swiss Bobs. The Swiss Bobs was our favorite, because all the girls stood and watched the bravest boys ride what was the fastest ride at the carnival, and because they cranked "The Joker" by Steve Miller from the control booth. The last night of the carnival always fell on the Fourth of July, and ended with a fireworks show that could be seen from most houses within a few miles of Dolton Park.

With Eddy's little bankroll in hand we hopped onto our bikes and headed toward the park. I had four dollars, enough for a few rides and a snow cone. We ditched our bikes among the trees and shrubs near the football field, and made our way toward the rides. Eddy reached into his pocket and pulled out a wad of single dollar bills, a few silver dollars and a mound of change.

"Here, take five," Eddy said, offering up a handful of crumpled singles and some change.

"Man, I can't take your money. Your mom gave it to you. I'll let you know if I run out, or you can buy a few ride tickets with it," I replied.

We made our way toward the games, starting with our favorite: the cane toss. All the coolest kids at the carnival walked around with colored wooden walking canes, won by throwing little plastic shower rings around the cane of your choice. It only took us a few tries each to win canes, and Eddy high-fived me after trading in two regular canes for one with two plastic dice at the top. Eddy beamed with pride and drew looks from all the other kids as we strutted through the carnival with our canes. Next we shot water pistols in the mouths of little plastic clown faces in order to inflate balloons that popped to pronounce the winner. After several tries Eddy won a small key chain with a red dragon dangling from it. I figured maybe left-handed kids were more coordinated than the rest of us. Eddy was good at every game we played, and while I held only my cane Eddy had already won a handful of stuffed animals and other cool stuff. He said he planned to give the stuffed animals to his girlfriend who still lived in Chicago. As we walked toward the rides he told me all about her, how pretty she was, that she was going to be a model when she grew up, and how she would soon be visiting him.

"Let's hit the Tilt-o-Whirl," I said. We screamed as we spun around and around, and we both daringly took our hands off the handle bar to get the full effect of the ride. It was the best carnival day I had ever had.

Dizzy and giddy with laughter, we stumbled off the ride and pretended to be drunk as we walked through the crowd. People looked at us like we were nuts, but we didn't care. We decided to buy a few Bozo's hot dogs with everything on them and orange slurpies. Eddy insisted on paying for everything. We ate, hit a few more rides, and then decided to head home to play catch. I was exhilarated by the games, rides and food, and wanted every trip to the carnival to be just like today. It wasn't just the usual thrill of a carnival that any kid would feel. It was being there with Eddy, my best friend. Seeing him happy and carefree. It was one of those rare perfect days that camps in your mind for years to come, and which shines even brighter after a close friendship abruptly ends.

"You didn't win any prizes, Mike," Eddy said. "Here, have my dragon key chain."

"Nah. I don't need anything. I had fun anyway. I've got my cane at least," I said raising the little blue stick over my head like a warrior preparing for battle. Eddy drew his cane and we jousted in circles a bit pretending to be expert fencers. Eddy struck a fatal stab to my heart and I fell to the ground in an exaggerated moan, doing my best impersonation of a dying knight in armor. Lying on the ground with my eyes closed, I heard Eddy say, "Hold on a minute. Wait here." I looked up to see him running back toward one of the booths. I waited by our bikes and he came back a few minutes later with a Chicago Cubs tee shirt.

"Here," Eddy said as he handed me the shirt.

"What's this for?"

"You can have it. My mom said to make sure I treat you, and I had a few dollars left over."

"Wow. Are you sure? This is really cool. I can't wait to wear it to school. Thanks!" We hopped on our bikes and headed home.

As we pulled up in front of Eddy's house, I noticed Richard standing on the front porch with his arms crossed, looking as he did the day he shooed Eddy inside. Sammy was sitting on the front lawn drawing stick figures in a patch of dirt, mumbling to himself. We stopped our bikes and I noticed Eddy's expression change when he spotted Richard. Before he was spoken to, he looked at Richard defensively and said, "What?"

Sammy muttered, "Eh-dee. Trubl. Steely mohney. Ed-dee. No steely mohney."

"Mom gave it to me," Eddy said unconvincingly, almost below his voice and avoiding eye contact with Richard.

"Michael, you need to head home," Richard said to me without looking my way. He stared at Eddy and I could tell he was pissed. I knew there was going to be trouble, so I slowly walked my bike off their lawn and down the sidewalk toward my house. As I turned to look back, Eddy dropped his bike and ran for his life through the side yard toward his back fence. In a single leap, Richard flew off the porch after Eddy, pulling his belt off his pants in one motion, dangling it from his right hand like a snake. As Richard flew by Eddy's brother toward the back yard, Sammy covered his ears, tucked his head between his legs and began to scream, "No hit Eh-dee. No hit my broda." And from two houses down, the thwack of Richard's belt against Eddy and a horrible wailing echo were the last sounds I heard before running through my front door.

At that point in my life I did not know any kids whose parents were divorced. It just wasn't too common back then. With the way Richard treated Eddy, I somehow equated people who got divorced and remarried as being not only out of place, but bad. Richard and

Barbara met at the Jewel Food Store on 82nd street in Chicago where they both worked. Prior to marrying Eddy's mom, Richard spent his weekends on Lake Michigan on his boat, which he kept docked at the Calumet Yacht Club on the south side of Chicago. I think the idea of moving in with Barbara and combining their incomes appealed to Richard, who was hoping to enjoy his retirement from twenty years in the Army with his second career at Jewel and lots of time on his boat with Barbara. But perhaps he underestimated going from having no kids to fathering three. Seemingly, he hedged his bet of his enjoyment of Barbara and their time together against the rigor and pressures of a mortgage and three young kids including one with special needs. And when the bet didn't pay dividends, he took it out on them.

There were times when I saw a softer, more caring side of Eddy's stepfather. Him sitting on the porch reading the newspaper, talking to other neighbors or offering to help them do a chore, trying to show Sammy how to ride his bike. It was obvious he was trying his best to make his new life with Barbara and the kids work out. Likely his father was stern and strict with him, providing him the only model he knew for how to be a father to his new family. Heck, most parents back then were highly directive with their kids. You did things because your parents "said so." There was limited debate on who was in charge.

Richard's job pressures were significant. As a Jewel manager he was responsible for hiring, training, supervision, purchasing and inventory, and advertising and security. Going from having complete freedom to having lots of responsibility was not insignificant financially or emotionally for him. In his mind, he was doing the best he could. Being firm with the kids was good for them. It was the way he was raised and how kids should be raised. And it would help them later in life. Richard rationalized that he was giving them the structure they lacked before he came along, and it was his contribution as their new father and his way of helping Barbara.

A few days later I asked my Mom if she knew what happened about the carnival money, and she said Barbara told her that Eddy took the money out of Richard's wallet without asking after she had already given him a few dollars of her own money for the carnival. I felt guilty that I was complicit in spending Richard's money, but each time Eddy took a beating from his stepdad, I became more distrustful and resentful toward Richard. I didn't like being in their house, even to step in the doorway a few minutes to wait for Eddy. It gave me the creeps, and I usually waited outside when I went over to ask Eddy to come outside to talk or play catch.

Eddy seemed to always be in trouble, even when he wasn't doing anything wrong. But sometimes Eddy's stepdad, who he later called "Hitler," took things a bit too far. My dad reprimanded us a bit, even yelled at times, but even the threat of a spanking was enough to get my brothers and I back in line. Unlike Eddy, we never lived in fear.

"Eddy, get to the store and bring back a loaf of bread and a carton of milk for your mother. Be on your way, mister, and hurry right back," Richard said while Eddy and I played catch in front of his house one morning about a month after the carnival incident. We didn't mind the interruption, since this meant getting to go to Panazzo's convenience store and picking up a few pieces of Bazooka gum with the spare change. We were already sweating in the August morning heat, so a break to ride to the store was perfect.

Eddy's bike was broken again, so he hopped on my handlebars and we made it there just as fast. We got the items Richard requested, and I bought us each a juice box and some gum. As we made the trip back and were within a few blocks of home, we came upon a group of kids playing a pick-up game of Nerf football in the street. Nerf was a cool spongy ball that had just come on the market that was easy to catch and could be thrown just as far as a real football. We knew most of the kids playing, and Eddy asked if they needed two more.

"What about your dad though? He seemed like he was in a hurry for us to get back," I said as we dismounted my bike.

"It's ok. He'll be fine. We'll just play for a few minutes," Eddy replied.

"Mike's on our team," Scott, a guy I knew from school, declared.

The only thing kids have less sense about than obeying their parents is having a sense of time. On this day we were bankrupt of both. A few minutes became a few games, probably over an hour since Richard handed Eddy two dollars and distinctly told him to come right home.

We got back on my bike sweaty from running in the mid-morning heat, Eddy holding the carton of milk and me holding the loaf of bread. We pulled around to Eddy's side gate and his dad was kneeling down beside their Weber grill, removing the greasy metal spit used to rotate meat cooked over charcoal. I handed Eddy the bread and he entered his gate and said, "I'll call you later." This time Richard didn't wait for me to leave to enact his anger toward Eddy. His rage didn't permit such discretion. Instead it rendered him oblivious to everything and everyone in his world except Eddy. He sprung up, grabbed Eddy by the back of the hair with one hand and walloped him on the back of his legs with the iron barbeque spit. The first strike brought Eddy quickly to his knees, his eyes rolling up toward the sky in pain. The carton of milk flew high into the air, exploding like a white bomb on the concrete porch, and Eddy reacted to the multiple violent blows by squeezing the loaf of bread so hard it crumbled into tiny pieces in midair.

"I fucking told you to come right back. Why can't you do a damn thing I ask you? How the hell am I supposed to drink warm milk!" Richard screamed as he smacked Eddy with the iron rod, this time on the small of his back, then threw it to the ground as he flung open the back door and threw Eddy inside like a ragdoll. I didn't witness the beating that continued inside, but heard the commotion from the front of the house as I hurried home. As I parked my bike and stood alone beside it, hot tears rolled off my chin and splattered on the garage floor like raindrops on dry pavement. Eddy was my best friend, and it was hard to watch him get beat up by the person who was supposed to love and protect him. Even at my age I knew this was wrong, yet I was powerless to make it stop.

That was the worst beating I saw Richard give Eddy, though I knew others took place. I could tell by the bumps and bruises on Eddy's arms and legs. But Richard seemed more careful from that day forward not to lash out at Eddy in public. He was usually careful not to go off on him in front of the neighbors, and I doubt he wanted a reputation as an abusive parent. But it was also obvious, even to me as a kid, that he couldn't control his temper.

Only a few weeks later I was getting ready for bed on a school night, and a series of loud knocks came at our front door. By the time I entered the living room, Mom had already answered and Eddy and Sammy were standing in the doorway in their pajamas.

"Momma, dada fitin. Mom dad fitin agin," Sammy repeated over and over, as he did with most of his sentences, reciting things like he would for the teachers in school to try to learn to talk. Living only two doors down from Eddy and his family, we grew accustomed to our ringside seats to the many family fights they had. When I asked my Mom how we could help, her reply was always a similar version of the same thing: "Stay out of it. It's none of our business."

Over time, I didn't worry as much about what went on inside Eddy's house. It was what it was. I sort of blocked it out and focused on the fun we had. If Eddy's life inside his house was going to be bad, I did my best to help life outside his house be good. My parents yelled at my brothers and me, often threatening to spank us. But at best this just instilled in us enough sense to straighten up and watch our words. Being afraid of catching my dad's hand on occasion and living in constant fear aren't the same. I lived one reality, Eddy lived another.

Everyone in our neighborhood rode motocross bicycles. It was 1975, and the motocross fad was nearing its peak. There were lots of hot bikes on the market, but the Redline was top dog. Alloy breaks, bright red bubble rims, knobby racing tires, fluted seat rod, dual breaks and Ashtabula gooseneck. We saw pictures of the Redline in magazines, and one hung in the window of Mr. Ed's Bike Shop in downtown Dolton. But no one owned one. Even the basic model was $80, and no one had that kind of money to spend, especially on a kid's bike.

Eddy always bragged about stuff we never saw him do. Like fishing for Coho on Lake Michigan with Richard (we never saw the fish), like having a girlfriend from his old neighborhood in Chicago (I never met her nor saw pictures of her), and like telling all the kids on the block he was going to be the first to get a Redline. No one really believed him. Behind his back the other kids said he was full of shit, and they avoided Eddy because there appeared to be something dishonest about him. Something that took too much time to figure out and rationalize. Or their parents simply told them to avoid Eddy and his family. But for some reason my mind put it all together for me in a way that made it ok. I knew Eddy was bragging about stuff that wasn't true because it was all he had. I knew once the neighborhood kids and I went home for the night after hanging out all day, the best part of Eddy's day was over, and the remaining part was terrible. Somehow this enabled me to give him a pass on all his lies.

Then one day it happened.

"Wow! Whose bike is that?" I asked Eddy as I answered my front door to find him standing there smiling from ear to ear, the brand new Redline parked at the base of my porch behind him shining like the '67 Corvettes we watched roll by in the Dolton Parade.

"It's mine. My mom bought it for me."

"No way. Don't even. Are you lyin'?"

Just then Eddy's mom walked over from their house, having partly overheard our conversation as she was heading to her car.

"Eddy, make sure you don't leave it out front if you go into Mike's house. If it gets stolen your father will kill me." The phrase hung in the air briefly enough for me to understand it was a figure of speech, but long enough for me to actually picture Richard doing some horrible act to Eddy's mom just because his new bike got stolen. Barbara looked more relaxed than I usually saw her, appearing immensely happy to see Eddy beaming with pride as the first kid on the block to own the bike of all bikes.

Seeing the new Redline confirmed it—this time Eddy had told the truth and made good on one of the things he promised would happen. Something beautiful found its way into his battered life. I later learned that Barbara had saved a little bit of her alimony check every month to eventually surprise Eddy for his birthday. It wasn't going to heal the bumps and bruises from Richard, but it likely made her feel a little less guilty about subjecting Eddy to Richard's strict parenting methods and exposing him to harm.

I hopped on my bike, feeling inferior but proud to be cruising with someone riding the best racing bike on the market, and we rode for hours and hours. In kid terms, this was like cruising a new Mustang on the main strip, pulling up to stop lights to the envy of other kids sitting in their beat up Pintos and Fairmonts. Other kids' mouths dropped as we rode by their houses, and several hopped on their bikes to chase us just to get a closer look at the Redline, pointing at it in awe.

A few weeks passed and Eddy seemed to really be mindful to take care of the bike. Maybe giving him some responsibility would be good for him, his parents probably thought. He let me take it for a few jumps off the dirt ramp which formed at the edge of the ice rink made each winter at the park. It was a thing of beauty and, unlike its owner, was thus far unblemished and unscratched. It appeared indestructible.

It was after Labor Day, and Eddy seemed to be making friends at school as the new kid. The girls liked him because he was cute, the guys liked him because he was a good athlete, and he made the other kids laugh because he was such a goofball to be around. Plus, he built up everything to be bigger than life, and padded everything with his usual exaggeration and bullshit. "I'm going to start racing as soon as my mom buys me a helmet. That black Bell helmet in Mr. Ed's window…"

"My mom is signing me up for football. I'll probably play quarterback since I'm the fastest kid in school…"

"Richard is taking me around the horn on Lake Michigan this weekend, so we'll be out on the boat for a few days catching fish and hanging out…"

Most days Eddy and I came home from school, played catch in his side yard, and then rode our bikes around the neighborhood. One day we noticed Richard hammering away behind their house, and it appeared he was building a shed in the back corner of their yard.

By November the shed was finished, and Eddy and I began spending most days after school playing hockey at the rink at the park up the block. My Mom had given me permission to give Eddy my old Bauer skates because he didn't own a pair. Eddy was thankful, but reminded me frequently that his mom was any day now about to buy him a new pair of CCM Tacks professional skates, just like the Chicago Blackhawks wore.

When it was colder than usual outside, we would break from skating and sneak a pack of matches from the house to light a fire in the alley adjacent to the rink. It was mid-December, and one of the coldest nights yet that winter. The wind howled and cut right through us as we skated.

"Shit. I'm freezing my ass off. If we can't warm up I'm heading home," I said.

"Follow me," Eddy said. "I have an idea."

We walked up the alley and arrived behind Eddy's house. It was dark inside, and we hopped his back fence and huddled behind his shed to protect us from the wind. Crouched down against the side of the shed, we cleared the snow and ignited the last several matches in the pack, first lighting a few dry leaves, then adding some scraps of paper we pulled from a nearby trash can, then an empty beer box. Soon we had a nice, toasty fire going.

"Shit, it's a good thing we got this going. It's freakin' freezing out here!" I said as I rubbed my hands together near the flames as they licked the cold night air.

"Michael, dinner!" my Mom shouted from our back door. As all the kids in our neighborhood did, when our parents yelled out the door for dinner we made our way home.

We stomped out the fire and Eddy headed back to the park to skate some more while I went in to eat.

"I'll try to come back out after dinner if my mom will let me," I said as I hurried home. I hopped my fence and kicked by skates off before heading inside.

As I ate supper, the warmth of being inside coupled with the start of the Andy Griffith Show extinguished my desire to go back out to skate in the cold. But as I scraped my plate into the trash I could hear the sound of fire engines in the distance. First faint, then louder and louder, as though they were right on our block.

My Mom grabbed her coat and ran out the back door. "Wait here. I'll be back after I find out what's happening."

As Mom headed out, I ran to our kitchen window. I could see part of Eddy's yard, but I didn't need to look to know what was going on. The orange glow and plumes of smoke from the shed told the story.

Two fire trucks pulled through the alley, and within minutes were pumping water onto the flaming shed. Richard kept the lawnmower, gas cans, and all their wooden yard tools in there. Its plywood floor, wooden studded frame and cedar shingled siding made for about as flammable a structure as one could build.

When my Mom came home I was crying, and told her I was with Eddy when the fire started, and how it all happened, and for the first and only time in my life I tasted a ration of what Eddy got a few times a week. The smack of my mom's hand on my butt was the smallest penance to pay for my role in the incident. I wished for more though, wanting his portion of the beating I knew he'd get. I wanted more than anything to wind back the clock and make a different decision about how to stay warm that evening. But I couldn't. That night I cried on my pillow for what we did to Richard's shed. I cried for the sting of my rump. And I cried out of worry for what would happen to Eddy at the hands of Richard. Then a horrible thought entered my mind, which caused me to lose my breath and stop crying momentarily. I remembered where Eddy stored the Redline.

When I first saw Jimmy Thoreau I wasn't overly impressed. I begrudgingly joined my Dad to watch my older brother's wrestling meet. I was in seventh grade, my brother in eighth, and our school, Lincoln Junior High, was wrestling Dirksen. My parents signed my brother up for wrestling when he was really young, maybe eight years old. He was short and stocky, so they figured this would be a good sport for him. He was also a pretty hyper kid, and I think they figured it would help him work off some of his aggression and burn off his nervous energy. Thinking back though, all the guys I hung out with as kids were "hyper." Unlike today, none of us got stuck in therapy or were forced to take medication. We were energetic little boys. We just worked it out.

Jimmy was no different. The smallest kid on the Dirksen wrestling team and only in seventh grade, Jimmy was a bit of a show-off. I didn't know much about wrestling at the time, but on this night Jimmy came onto the mat, and the whistle blew to start the match. Within ten seconds he pinned his opponent and stood pumping his fists in the air like an Olympic champion. The crowd went wild, and I thought he was a bit of a ham to do that at the expense of the other kid. My brother also won his match that night, using a move called a Japanese Whizzer to pin his opponent in the first period. "Japanese Whizzer." Sounded mystical. *What a cool name for a wrestling move,* I thought.

45

I continued to go with my Dad to watch my older brother's wrestling meets, and though they had signed me up for basketball—mostly because, unlike my brother, I was tall and thin—something about the sport of wrestling appealed to me. There was no reliance on teammates to succeed or fail. Each match was one-on-one, won by the person who could score more points by taking the other guy down or pinning his shoulder blades to the mat for three seconds. Figuring out how to do so took technique, speed, and strength.

The following year I tried out for Lincoln's team and made the squad. I worried that most of the other kids, like my brother, had been doing it for years and would be much better than me. But only a few had wrestled before. Most were actually just experimenting with the sport for the first time. I won my first match 13-0 against a fish. In wrestling, if you really stink they call you a fish, because you sort of just flop around on the mat like a fish out of water. But as the season went on and we competed against better teams, even my raw enthusiasm for the sport didn't help me against the better wrestlers who had already been grappling for a few years.

The day came for us to compete against Dirksen Junior High. It was commonly held that my school, Lincoln, was better than Dirksen in most sports. But Jimmy and some of the other kids who had wrestled in the park district league before middle school now wrestled for Dirksen. With my brother Dave now a freshman over at Thornridge, a lot of Lincoln's talent had moved on.

Weigh-ins at wrestling matches are pretty bizarre. Each team lines up in front of a scale, the same scale you hop onto at the doctor's office when you get a physical, only every kid in line is stripped down totally naked. The first time I experienced this I was a little freaked out. But, other than seeing kids with uncircumcised penises for the first time, I got used to it.

Starting with the lowest weight class, 98 pounds, each wrestler gets on the scale and his weight is announced to a referee (enjoying the luxury of standing between the scales with clothes on I might add). If both players are under their weight limit, they approach each other between the scales and shake hands. Shaking hands in the nude with opponents I'd never met before took some getting used to. If the wrestler is overweight, which always pissed the coaches off, he had thirty minutes to put on a rubber suit, run off a pound or two, and then return for a second weigh-in. This is called "making weight." Once everyone made weight, we could go pig out before the meet started. Most kids were starving by then, so they would bring bags of food and gorge themselves in the locker room after weigh-in. Not very healthy in retrospect, but it always gave me an appreciation of how good food tasted. Most nights after practice I had a bowl or rice and glass of iced tea for dinner. Wrestlers got the short end of the stick when it came to eating (compared to football players who could eat as much as they wanted to). But the beauty of the sport is that it is one of the few that is totally body-oriented. No equipment other than the body and the brain, and no teammates to bail you out or bring you down. Other than boxing, it is one of only a few individual contact sports.

As my luck would have it, Jimmy was in the same weight class as I was. I didn't realize this before the match, and my brother didn't mention it to me even though he wrestled against Jimmy on the park district team for years and probably knew he was around the same weight as me. I think he didn't want to psych me out. Come weigh in, there was Jimmy, 98 pounds of muscle and a foot shorter than me, lined up ready to kill, snickering with his teammates and pointing in my direction, sizing me up. After dismounting the scales we met in the middle to shake hands, and Jimmy looked me in the eye and said, "You're Walker's little brother. I haven't decided whether to stick you like a fish or take it easy on you." I wanted to offer up some well thought-out reply, but none came to mind. This was probably better, as I was already scared to death and didn't want to make matters worse.

Our weight class was the first match, and as I was stretching on the side of the mat my brother came out of the bleachers and over to talk to me.

"Alright. You know this guy is a stud. He hasn't lost a match in two years. When you shake his hand, say something funny to him and try to make him laugh. If he thinks you're a goofball, he'll just take it easy on you and win the match by points. If he thinks you think you can win and try to give him a match, he'll rip your head off."

"Great," I replied. "Like what should I say?" Then the whistle blew and the ref called us onto the mat. Over the applause of the audience as I hustled to the center circle of the mat, I barely heard my brother's reply in the distance, "You'll think of something!"

I took off my warm up jersey and felt nearly as naked as I did at the weigh-in, my skinny frame and inexperience in the sport exposed for all to see. Our uniforms were a "singlet," which is a tight pair of shorts connected to a bib covering the stomach and chest hung by thin shoulder straps. I looked like a stick figure that might snap with the slightest amount of pressure applied to any body part. Jimmy ran onto the mat to toe the line. *What the hell am I doing here?* I thought to myself. *Why didn't I just stick with basketball?*

I jogged onto the mat, and before the ref approached us to start the match I looked at Jimmy and said, "I had a great time with your sister last night." The whistle blew and the match was on.

The following year at Thornridge High School as freshmen, Jimmy and I were assigned the same homeroom and had a few classes together. He lived only a block from me, so most mornings we walked to school together. Jimmy's sister Kari was three years older than us, and she and their mom came to all Jimmy's matches together. Jimmy's parents divorced years ago, and his father lived in another state.

Jimmy and I also hung out outside of wrestling. We goofed around at parties, and one night we pushed a water hose through a kid's basement screen window and turned it on after the kid refused to let us into his keg party. We could always be seen hanging out in the hallway between classes, teasing other kids as they passed, and we played hockey at the park nearly every night in the winter. Jimmy was shorter than I, so proportionally he had a stockier build. Girls whispered and pointed at him as he walked the Thornridge hallways. Even as a freshman he fit in with most of the cliques in school. The jocks respected him, the preppy kids liked him, and the burnouts always saw him at the weekend parties. Everyone knew he was the best wrestler in the school, and he commanded the respect of the teachers, was the envy of the guys, and drew great attention from the hottest girls. In my eyes, Jimmy had it made.

By the time wrestling season came around, the hype surrounding Jimmy's promise as a wrestler was huge. He was selected pre-season all conference by the *Chicago Tribune*, rumored to be able to compete with the best wrestlers in his weight class from schools that placed in the state tournament the year before—Mt.

Carmel, Marist and Thornwood. But Jimmy took it all in stride. It came easy to him, and he didn't really need to work at it. He did just enough to get by in practice, relying more on his natural ability and years of experience wrestling since he was a little kid. He toyed with his opponents like Michael Jordan did on the court, always with another gear in store as necessary. In the locker room before practice Jimmy stripped down to only his jock strap, stood on the bench in front of his locker with his arms raised like Rocky Balboa, and yelled out, "Adrian!" The seniors thought he was nuts.

Coach Marino, all five feet, ten inches and 210 pounds of contained fury, yelled out across the practice room as we stretched at the start of practice.

"This is not basketball, ladies. This is where we separate the men from the boys! If you aren't prepared to commit yourself to becoming a champion, leave now, go home and play Atari with your sister!"

The practices were hell. Twenty minutes of stretching, agility drills, and rigorous calisthenics, then thirty minutes of staggered jogging and sprints through long hallways and up and down stairwells, then thirty minutes of live scrimmaging against opponents at the same or a heavier weight class. Practices ended with twenty minutes of paced weight training, doing high repetitions with increasingly heavier weights. Most guys sweated off five pounds in practice alone, and we weren't permitted more than a few sips of water until practice was over. But the harder we worked, the tougher it made us.

Jimmy and I usually paired up in practice to scrimmage, and I was amazed at how good he was. Whatever move I tried to place on him, he automatically countered. His brain didn't need to tell his body how to react. Wrestling was totally instinctive to him. He denied it, but Jimmy always took it easy on me. He let me score an occasional take-down before slipping a half-nelson or cradling me up like a wad of paper. He was a natural, and wrestling against him in practice made me a better wrestler.

I gained a few pounds since eighth grade, knowing that I would need to compete for a starting position in a weight class other than Jimmy's. I didn't stand a chance of beating him in a wrestle off, which was the match at the last practice each week to determine who got to represent the team at that week's meet in each weight class.

Jimmy and I got a charge out of wearing our warm-up jerseys to school on days we had matches. I learned pretty quickly in high school that most kids thought the jocks were pretty cool, and that no one messed with the wrestlers. The kid whose locker was next to mine, Terry Kane, would sneak up behind me and jump on my back to see how quickly I could react and flip him onto the floor. Kane was in all the plays in school and could make anyone laugh on a moment's notice. He loved jostling with me and Jimmy in the hallway between classes, approaching us in his mock wrestler's stance until we tackled him and made him yell mercy.

So Jimmy represented us in the 98 pound weight class, and I was at 105. As the home matches started they cranked up the T'Ridge fight song over the loud speaker as we ran out onto the mat and circled it. "Onward, Onward Thornridge High. On to Victory Do or Die!" The crowd went nuts for this, and Jimmy and I honed in on the two wrestlerette cheerleaders we were most hot for. When the matches started they sat Indian-style on the side of the mat doing cheers, pounding their pom-poms on their knees. This always motived me not to lose. The only thing worse than losing a wrestling match is losing while a girl you like is watching.

Each match gave me a chance to watch Jimmy, to learn from him. I studied him with hopes of emulating his moves. But he was a masterful technician. Effortless. Poetry in motion. He seamlessly strung together moves before his opponent had time to react. A double leg takedown fluidly followed by a half nelson, followed by a cradle for a pin. A standup followed by a standing reverse connected with a takedown from behind. A single leg takedown then sinking the leg to a three-quarter nelson.

Wrestling to Jimmy Thoreau was innate. And every time the ref raised Jimmy's hand at the end of a match declaring him victor, I saw in his face a deep satisfaction. The kind of harmony that occurs when one knows, not thinks, he is good at something. The wrestling mat was his territory, his domain. Something he could control the outcome of. Jimmy was beautiful to watch but impossible to copy. I could do as he did no more than the average man could conduct the Boston Symphony.

But there was also something troubling about his relationship to the sport. An apparent resentment at a deeper level. It was subtle at first, but later became more obvious.

After five matches Jimmy was undefeated. I was 3-2. The coming weekend was a big meet against rival Thornwood, the rich kids who lived in neighboring South Holland. I was pretty nervous, but Jimmy showed no fear.

"I already beat the guy I'm wrestling three times in the Dolton Park league, so it's no big deal," Jimmy said. "You'll probably get thrashed though," he laughed as we left practice the day before the meet.

"Thanks a lot," I replied.

"Hey. My mom is going out Saturday night, so if we win I'm having a party at my house. My sister's boyfriend said he would buy me a keg and everything, so tell a few people and stop by."

As Jimmy predicted, he pinned his opponent in the first period, and I lost a closer than expected match to a solid black kid, 8-7. We won the meet, so the party was on. It was mid-January, and we just had the first decent snow of the season that afternoon. A guy I worked with at Bozo's Hot Dogs, a senior named Kurt, offered to pick up a few friends and me and bring us to Jimmy's party. Kurt was friends with Jimmy's sister, so Kurt, Jim Morgan, Terry Kane, Paul Lamb and I made our way to Jimmy's cramped in Kurt's VW bug. It was a piece of shit, but he loved cruising it down Dolton's alleys, plowing over as many trash cans as possible. The best thing about going to parties with Kurt was that he was one of the biggest, toughest guys in our school. Between him and my older brother Dave, no one ever screwed with us.

By the time we got to Jimmy's house there were already around twenty-five other kids there, some from the wrestling team, some from Kari's gymnastics team, and other kids from the neighborhood just looking for beer. Most of the kids there paid Kari's boyfriend $2 for a cup to drink beer from the keg. Our cups were free. Nothing like standing in a freezing cold garage in the dead of a Chicago winter, listening to Free Bird and drinking draft beer.

I filled my cup with what seemed like one big head of foam, and looked up to see Jimmy entering the garage. Man he was in good shape. He smiled and ran over to tussle with the guys I was standing with.

"Hey Walks. Nice match today. You almost had him," Jimmy said, giving me a friendly fist to the chest.

"Yeah. That freakin' ref wouldn't give me extra back points in the third period. I think he figured since I threw that hip toss in the final minute I was just lucky to be in the match at all. I was getting pummeled for two periods. How's the party?" I said as I blew foam onto his garage floor and tried to pump legitimate beer into my cup.

"Cool. I'm hoping a few more girls will show up so it isn't a total sausage-fest. Have fun man, but don't fucking steal anything. If any of my sister's friends screw with you, tell them to piss off."

As Morgan pumped beer into his cup, Kurt made his way over to talk to a few older kids. Morgan peered over the rim of his beer at Sandy Franklin, a girl from the neighborhood who, like Morgan, was a hard-bodied gymnast and who was smiling back at him. Dark hair, brown eyes, and a muscular and curvy body, she was outside the league of most other freshmen. She didn't seem to be with a guy, standing next to her friend Eileen. Eileen was cute but seemed a bit quirky, so I tried not to make eye contact with her. I could tell Morgan was honing in on Sandy though.

"Walks, I'm going to go talk to Sandy," Morgan said. "I met her at gymnastics practice this season and I think she's into me. She's pretty hot, isn't she?"

"Dude, no way you're hooking up with her. Anyway, I highly doubt she's into you. But tell her we're in a rock band...and see if she has any hot friends."

"Whatever. If I can get her alone somewhere inside Jimmy's house, just keep an eye out for me."

"Great. I'll just stand out here freezing my ass off. Have fun."

Jim made his way toward Sandy and Eileen and struck up a conversation. After a few minutes they slipped out of the garage and toward Jimmy's house. I noticed Eileen getting ready to make her way toward me; this was my cue to head inside to warm up. A few minutes later I found myself immersed in a mean game of Asteroids in Jimmy's living room, adjacent to his bedroom. All of a sudden, Jimmy's mom blasted through the front door, clearly agitated that her house was filled with kids hanging out and swilling beer.

"James Thoreau! Where the hell are you?" his mom yelled, throwing her purse down and scanning the living room.

"Hey Ms. Thoreau," I said, as she headed directly toward Jimmy's bedroom. She liked me, but my salutation had no effect on reducing her agitation, nor altered her beeline toward Jimmy's bedroom. She assumed Jimmy was shacked up with some girl inside. When it suddenly dawned on me that Morgan and Sandy might be getting it on in Jimmy's bedroom, I jumped off the couch and tried to head her off.

"He's not in there! He's in the garage!"

But this awkward interception made her all the more curious, so she threw open Jimmy's bedroom door and flipped on the light. I heard a lamp crash to the floor and a girl scream, then Jimmy's mom bellowed, "What the hell is going on here? Who are you? Get your damn clothes on and get outta here!"

In a flash Morgan streaked out of the room fully naked, holding his clothes over his mid-section, followed by Sandy with only a bra on and attempting to pull her jeans up as she stumbled out of the room and through the living room past a roomful of astonished, beer-buzzed teenagers laughing their asses off. Jimmy's mom came out, and we scattered like roaches. The night ended the same way most of Jimmy's wrestling matches did—early.

By the end of freshman year I was reduced to junior varsity. Jimmy and our group were partying on weekends instead of staying in shape and training, and I couldn't keep up with the more dedicated opponents. Unlike Jimmy, I wasn't a natural born athlete. My body required complete dedication and training in order to compete; his didn't. Jimmy was undefeated by the time the conference tournament rolled around at the end of the season, and ranked fourth in the state among all 98-pounders. The wins came easy to him, though Marino knew he wasn't devoting enough time toward getting ready for the conference tournament. I think he suspected Jimmy was partying hard and slacking on his training.

"Jimmy, you can't walk on both sides of the street," Marino said as he followed us up to the practice room. "If you want to be a winner, you'll have to make some sacrifices. Decide whether you want to be a state champion or just another decent wrestler. Stop fucking around and get after it, son."

Turns out Coach was right. Jimmy made it to the finals of the conference tournament, then lost 6-2 to a senior from Crete. The following weekend's state qualifying tournament yielded a similar result. Jimmy lost in the second round 8-5, and would not advance to the state tournament at the University of Illinois the following weekend.

Having sat through each match to root him on, we talked in the locker room after his final match.

"Dude, you did great. Just couldn't keep him off you long enough to set up another take down," I said to Jimmy as he lay on his back on the concrete floor in front of his locker. He was breathing heavy and appeared totally gassed.

"I could care less. I'm only wrestling to make my mom happy. It's the only thing she gets to brag about. I'm already sick of doing it since I started when I was seven. I can't imagine having to go through three more years of practices and matches. Fuck this."

"Man, you're like one of the best wrestlers in Chicago. Besides, next summer you and Rodenberg and me talked about going up to Michigan for wrestling camp. Don't you want to go to state next year to..." but Jimmy interrupted.

"You're not listening to me, Walks. I don't want it anymore. I may do it one more year, but after that I'll probably fake an injury or just do something stupid to get thrown off the squad. I just want to hang out and have fun."

I let it go at that, figuring maybe he was just tired after a long season and pissed that he wasn't going to the state tourney.

Several weeks later my mom woke me early on a Saturday morning to give me the news.

As time went on, Eddy and I hung out less frequently. We attended different middle schools but still played baseball and hockey at the park. Eddy began hanging out with kids who smoked cigarettes, drank alcohol and smoked pot. By the time we started high school, we didn't spend nearly as much time together as when we were kids. I got into wrestling and Eddy was rarely seen in school at all. Sometimes from two doors down I could hear Eddy and Richard yelling at each other, and I knew that Eddy's tolerance for his stepdad's abuse grew shorter as he grew older and stronger. I would sometimes see Eddy at parties in high school, and we would share a beer and reminisce about old times: sneaking beers out of the fridge and chugging them behind my garage, peeking at Richard's

Playboy collection, cruising the Redline when it was brand new, and burning Hitler's shed to the ground. And like most meaningful childhood friendships, Eddy and I shared a bond that even our separate social circles couldn't break. He was a touchstone of my youth that I could always come back to for comfort and memories.

By the time I started college, I had mostly lost touch with Eddy. Mom said he moved out of the house and took a job working midnights down at the boat yard. She said he got tired of fighting with Richard and protecting his mom and Sammy from Richard's abuse. Sandy had long ago moved in with a guy a few towns over.

It was the end of final exam week my sophomore year when the house phone at my fraternity rang. I had just awakened and was having breakfast in the kitchen with the guys. I hung onto the phone and my mom's words until I recognized what they meant. Then the glass of juice I was holding slipped through my hands and hit the floor, shattering into pieces much like Eddy's body did when it flew through the window of his car. Heading home from his shift with a few buddies after stopping for some beers, he crossed the median and hit a forty-five year-old father of two head on. Eddy, his two passengers, and the man in the opposing car were all dead on the scene.

I made it home just in time for the viewing, and struggled to approach the casket to view the body of my best friend from childhood. I felt sorry for him, his life over at nineteen. I flashed through the good times we shared. Daily bouts of playing catch, pretending we were the starting pitcher and catcher for the Chicago Cubs, playing hockey at the park each winter and tackle football each fall. Eddy was as fearless on the playing field as he was confronting his demons at home. The funeral parlor was crowded, mostly with kids we went to high school with and people Eddy's mom and stepdad worked with. I spotted Richard and intentionally avoided talking to him. Somehow I blamed him for Eddy's death, while also feeling a sense of relief that Eddy would no longer need to experience the pain that his family life inflicted on him.

I skipped the funeral, though Barbara invited me to be a pall bearer, choosing instead to head out drinking with my brothers and a few of Eddy's friends. He wouldn't want us wringing our hands and crying over him. He would want us smiling up at him and telling him to take it light. At the end of the night we raised our glasses to

Eddy, and at the top of our lungs shouted like drunken sailors the poem he taught us to recite to our parents over and over just to piss them off:

"My name is Yon Yonson, I come from Wisconsin, I work in a lumber mill there. When I walk down the street, all the people I meet, they say, hello, what's your name, and I say, My name is Yon Yonson, I come from Wisconsin, I work in a lumber mill there..."

"Michael. Are you up yet?" I wasn't sure if the voice was part of my dream or reality.

"Not really. I could sleep all day actually. What do you want?"

"Jimmy's mom was taken to the hospital last night, and I'm not sure if she is going to make it. Your father was on duty and mentioned it this morning. Just wanted to let you know."

"What?" I sprang up in bed. "What happened?"

"Don't know. Something about taking some pills or something."

I got out of bed and called Jimmy's house, and there was no answer. My Mom offered to give me a ride to Sibley Memorial Hospital where Jimmy's mom was being treated, and I made my way toward her room. In the waiting room I found Jimmy, Kari, and a few of their friends.

"Jimmy, man, you doing ok? What happened?"

"Hey Walks. Thanks for coming." Jimmy looked tired, like he had been crying, and handed his sister the cigarette he had been smoking.

"I got home after seeing a movie and found her on the kitchen floor. She was like turning blue or something, so I called 911 and they came and got her. She's been in there since midnight, and all they can say is they are running some tests to see what she took."

"Dude, I'm sorry. I'll hang here with you for a bit. Do you need anything?"

"No. I'm cool. But thanks for coming, man." Jimmy gave me a hug, which I wasn't expecting. He was not the type to show emotion. I could tell the whole thing with his mom hit him hard.

We hung out for a bit and the doctor came out and said that she was going to make it. He said she took a handful of pills and vodka and would need to stay in the hospital another night. I felt bad that Jimmy was having to deal with all this, and I wondered how much time he spent at home taking care of his mom instead of her taking care of him.

Jimmy and I continued to spend time together, but he also starting hanging out with some real losers. Then before long I noticed he wasn't around as much. At first it was subtle. He would cut me short on a phone call, or not reply to a note I would leave in his locker about making plans for the weekend. Then I would see him out at a party with a rough crowd, burnouts that treated everyone like shit and smoked pot in the parking lot between classes. He wrestled the next season, his sophomore year, but missed practices and argued a lot with Coach Marino. I could tell he was just going through the motions with no real desire to win, just as he predicted at the end of the previous season. He won the conference tournament his sophomore year, then lost in the second round at districts and again did not qualify for the state tournament. As Jimmy lost interest in wrestling, my interest increased.

I was bummed that we weren't both leading the team and focusing on winning matches together. My sophomore year I was runner up for the JV Conference Championship. During the off-season we drank every weekend and had a blast, both of us now with our licenses and cruising all over town. But when he wasn't with me, he was partying even harder with Kari's crowd.

Before the start of his junior season, Jimmy told coach he crashed on his dirt bike and messed up his knee, faking a limp whenever he passed Marino in the hallway. That was the end of Jimmy's once-promising wrestling career.

As Jimmy drifted away, I began spending time with a different crowd. Athletes, kids that wrote for the *Bagpipe* school newspaper, kids in the marching band, kids that were college-bound. I played drums in *A Funny Thing Happened on the Way to the Forum*, and Terry Kane introduced me around to a group of actors who drank but didn't go overboard with drugs and alcohol. And I stuck with wrestling for all four years.

In a school of talented athletes who dominated football and basketball, wrestling spoke to me because it kept me in great shape and motivated me to take my stress out in a productive way. I worked hard and improved each year. Though he was done with wrestling, I tried to stay close to Jimmy. In some ways I felt like the big brother he never had. I felt compelled to try to keep him on the right track. Besides, he was a blast to be around, he was still popular, and he always made me laugh.

Graduation night came and we all met at my house for a few beers before the ceremony. It was a beautiful, sunny day. We stood on my front lawn as our parents proudly took pictures. Jimmy's mom dropped him off but did not stay.

"What's up, Walks? Hard to believe high school is over," Jimmy said as we hugged and then he punched me in the chest as he always did.

"I know. These last two seasons weren't the same without you. Marino rode my ass hard, but he was pretty happy I stuck it out and finished all four years. I miss all the crazy shit you did in the locker room, and messing with your opponents. Remember the time you posed for a picture in the middle of a match? I think it was that fish from Thornton you had in a headlock? Man, Marino went ape shit!"

Jimmy chuckled and we went inside to put our caps and gowns on. I could tell from the glaze in his eyes he was high, so I handed him my sunglasses. "Here, these look good on you, Hollywood," I said as I winked at him.

After graduation, Jimmy took a job installing garage doors and signed up for some classes at Thornton Community College. We decided to meet at Nick's Sports Page bar a week before I was to leave for WIU. Jimmy had been seeing a girl named Monica a few years older than him he met running with Kari's crowed, but whenever they were together they were fighting about something or another. By the time they walked into the bar they were already going at it, and looked as though they were already wasted.

"Whazzup, Walks?! Big time college brain. Man, you better invite me to some parties down there so we can hang out and chase some college chicks!" Monica had already walked away from us to head to the bathroom.

"Yo. What's going on your way? Are you guys getting serious or what?"

"Hard to say. She's fun but she's always on my ass. But she likes to party which is cool."

"Dude, be careful with that shit. Get your ass in class and get a degree so you're not digging ditches the rest of your life, punk," I said as I returned Jimmy's patented chest punch to him. This made him smile, as he reached for a few beers off the bar.

"Screw digging ditches. I work for 'A Better Garage Door,'" he said sarcastically. "What a bunch of shit. Get this: last week I was at this guy's house installing a new garage door and he wasn't home. When I finished I had to take a dump something fierce. So I grab my empty brown lunch bag and am in his garage taking a shit. Wouldn't you know it—the guy surprises me and comes in the service door of the garage. Caught me red-handed taking a dump into a bag in his garage. Man, the look on his face!"

The vision of this made me roar, and we clinked bottles and talked for a while before Monica returned from the bathroom. I had a few beers and then had another party to go to, so I made my way toward the door. Jimmy and Monica were in the corner, deadlocked in another argument and having their usual drama, and she was flailing her arms about as she yelled at him about something. He turned his head my way and I motioned for him to come over.

"I need to head out. Give me a call this week so I can say bye to you and your mom before I leave for school. You cool?"

"Yeah man. Monica is pretty messed up already, and bitching about me looking at other girls. What a drag." I could tell Jimmy was really drunk by now, and it was only 9:30.

"Man, take it easy and just have fun. If you leave here later, stop by and see if I'm home and we'll hang out. Don't forget to call me this week so I can drop you one more time!" I put him in a playful headlock as I said this, and even in his drunken state he easily whisked me to the side. He still lifted weights and was in great shape, and the jostling reminded me of what a great wrestler he once was.

I stopped at a few other parties mostly to see some friends who were also leaving for college soon. It was around midnight when I drove down Lincoln Avenue to head toward my house, and saw all the police cars and fire trucks at the corner of Lincoln and Sibley. I would have kept driving, but the sight of Jimmy's smashed up Chevy Nova stopped me in my tracks. I knew most of the cops on the scene, so I jumped out toward the intersection where Jimmy's car was crumpled into a tiny mass of metal and glass, stuck partly under the trailer of a large service truck, which was also pretty mangled. No ambulance was there, so I figured they were just clearing the scene. I approached Officer Hammer, a friend of my dad's.

"Hammer, what happened? Where's Jimmy? Did they take him to the hospital already?"

"Who?"

"The guy who owns the Nova."

"Bad scene, man. Around eleven he blew through the red light, must have been doing 80, and hit the truck. Didn't even see him coming. The truck driver said another car, some girl by herself, passed through the intersection just before him and barely missed the truck. Seems he was chasing her."

"Monica probably. His girlfriend. Where is he, is he going to be ok?" By now the shock of the scene made my knees wobble a bit, and my stomach fluttered.

"Oh man, it wasn't even close. He was pinned into his dashboard with no seatbelt when we arrived. He's in the morgue already. DOA."

DOA. The initials hung in the night air for a second, then I felt light-headed and hit the ground. I couldn't believe it. I had just talked to him a few hours ago. Hammer helped me up and asked if I was ok to drive home.

"Sorry, Mike. You must have known him, huh? What a shame. So young."

I made my way back home in a trance, woke up my Mom and Dad, and told them the news. I didn't sleep that night, and as the sun was coming up I threw some shorts on and made my way back toward the Lincoln/Sibley intersection. Maybe it was all just a bad dream. I had to see whether there were any signs of the accident remaining. I had to see if Jimmy was really gone.

The morning was bright and sunny, a perfectly blue sky overhead. The intersection was still wet with whatever they used to spray down the gas and oil that leaked as a result of the accident. Thousands of tiny pieces of glass on the black asphalt street reflected in the sun like diamonds on a beach. As the traffic on Lincoln Avenue whizzed by, one piece of glass in particular caught my eye, glimmering directly in my sight and making me squint. I looked away, but every time I scanned the intersection my eyes were drawn to the same piece of glass sparkling brighter than the rest—like a roomful of school children with their hands up begging for the teacher to call on them, but one student raising his hand higher than the rest, waiving it harder and faster in order to be chosen. I reached down and picked it up, just as it was hoping I would. A fragment of what was left of my friend. I stood there holding the tiny jagged piece of glass and realized this was no dream. Jimmy was gone.

I walked back to my car and got in. Before I could start the engine, I gripped the steering wheel and rested my head against it, crying heavily. Three days later, the day before I left for college, I attended Jimmy's funeral. His mom hugged me and said, "Hi Michael. I wish he spent more time with you, and stayed with wrestling. He really looked up to you like a brother. I know you'll miss him."

I didn't recognize many of the people at the service. Lots of Kari's crowd and other kids Jimmy hung out with after he quit the wrestling team. Looked like a rough bunch, and a few kids dropped packs of cigarettes into the casket as they passed. I wanted to tell them Jimmy wouldn't need them where he was going. Didn't they realize he was dead? Monica was a total mess, and leaned on the shoulder of some guy trying to comfort her. I couldn't believe the crowd he hung with. I wondered whether I could have done more to keep him on track, kept him on the team where Marino's discipline would have been good for him. Marino's absence at the funeral was noticeable, but not surprising. He gave up on Jimmy years ago, just as Jimmy had given up on the sport that he was born for.

I made my way back to my car, got in, and glanced down at the glass fragment I had tossed into the empty ash tray after leaving the scene of the wreck. It was all I had to connect me to Jimmy, and as I picked it up it sparkled as though it was speaking on his behalf. *I know. It's cool, Walks. Don't worry. I'll be watching from up here. I've got one of God's angels in a head lock right now, and he's begging for mercy.*

Though Western didn't have a wrestling team, I entered the annual intramural wresting tournament for my fraternity that fall. I was in great shape, having decided to steer away from the crap that pulled Jimmy down. I wrapped the tiny glass fragment in a piece of tissue and taped it to my chest before the first match. With the

61

memory of Jimmy in my heart and thereby inheriting his strength and ability on the mat, I tore through the competition and won my weight class for the campus tournament. It was no consolation for Jimmy being gone, but it was the closest thing to honoring him that I could achieve. He may have lost his interest in wrestling mid-way through high school, but there was a time when he was phenomenal. When he was the one everyone talked about, and when everyone assumed he would be a multi-year state champion. On the bracket poster for my weight class that each tournament champion received, I scratched off my name and filled in "Jimmy Thoreau." The bracket remained on my wall all through college, giving me inspiration whenever the pressure of college got to be too much. I mailed the first place ribbon to Jimmy's mom with a short note: "This is for Jimmy. The best wrestler of all."

DOC

It wasn't as though I needed the job, though the extra money would help. I was saving up for a few more pieces for my drum set, bothered that Vince Lozano had the biggest, best set in school. His smarmy little Italian voice rang down the hallway as I left third period every Tuesday: "Walker, when are we going to battle?" I didn't care. I doubted he was better than me, but I sure as heck didn't want him to have the better drum set just the same.

When the offer came to work two evenings and one Saturday a week at the South Holland Animal Clinic, I was intrigued. Jeff Bonebrake from bell choir at church mentioned it a few times, and each time told me how cool it was to work at a place where you took care of dogs and cats, got to watch animal surgeries, and occasionally saw litters of puppies and kittens delivered.

"I promised Doc I would help him find another person to help out, so are you interested or not?" Jeff said, almost desperate for my answer as though somehow it was his own animal hospital, or he was getting a bonus for finding a new kid to work there.

"What do I need to do?" I asked.

"Pretty much clean the cages, mop the floors. The usual shitty work for low pay. If you can stop by today after school to meet Doc, he can fill you in from there. He's a really cool guy to work for, and it's a fun job."

"Sounds good. If it works out I'll need to make sure I can get the car a few nights a week, weekends are no problem, but I will be there today after school for sure."

I had no preconceived notion of what working at a veterinary hospital would be like. To that point I had worked only at Bozo's Hot Dogs, slinging weenies into buns a few evenings a week, cleaning up the place, etc. I also worked briefly at Chris' Coffee Shop off the highway, sweeping, mopping, and taking out the trash after hours. We always owned dogs as pets, first a mutt then a pair of German Shepherds. I wasn't a cat lover, my first experience with one being when my Grandma's cat Bootsie scratched my arm when I was a five. I had no desire to be a vet growing up. I actually had no inkling what I wanted to do later in life, I just knew that being around animals all day wasn't it. But Jeff was a pretty cool kid and I liked the idea of earning more money, so looking into the opportunity was a no brainer.

The South Holland Animal Clinic, or "SHACK" as it was known, was in the next town over from Dolton, about a 20 minute drive. I was somewhat familiar with its location, having played a few little league football games around the corner from the clinic as a kid. Even though I was only a sophomore, Mom and Dad were cool with me picking up another job and a little more cash to support my music habit. They were all about their kids being industrious, and my mom reminded me, "Save your money for college, Michael. You know your dad and I can only help you so much."

It was late spring, and I was surprised at how warm the lobby of the SHACK was when I entered the afternoon of my interview. Jeff was finishing up mowing the lawn as I walked in, and the smell of fresh cut grass filled the sun-lit lobby. The receptionist, Cathy, smiled and greeted me from behind the tall reception desk. From where I stood, all I could see was her head. As I approached the counter though, her bulging frame came into full focus.

"You must be Michael," she greeted me, big hand extended.

"Yes. Jeff told me to come talk to Dr. Dodson today about the kennel boy job."

Cathy giggled a bit, then replied, "Veterinary assistant, technically, or kennel kid as I like to say. I understand you go to church with Jeff. Doc has a few more appointments to see, so have a seat and he'll call you in shortly."

Cathy seemed nice, but was covered top to bottom with cat hair on her tan pants and white blouse. As I turned to take a seat, I noticed the beads of sweat that matted her black and graying hair against her forehead also held a layer of cat hair against her lily white skin, making her appear a bit like an overstuffed, balding lamb. I didn't want to blow my chances at landing the job though, so I sat down without cracking a grin or offering my observation about the cat hair. I later learned that Cathy was divorced and had a few snotty kids who disrespected her, and since working at SHACK adopted eight stray cats to go with the six she already owned. Seems in order to fill the enormous void in her life she scooped up every little furry feline that came through the place in need of a home. Before I was even offered the job, I already pictured myself spending extra time sweeping up lots of cat hair from under Cathy's desk. *Gross.*

A few ladies were seated in the lobby, one with a small black poodle on her lap, tongue hanging out and drooling onto the beige linoleum floor. An older woman in professional dress wearing lots of jewelry and with a yapping dog in a little box under her feet flipped anxiously through *Parade* magazine, appearing very put out and impressing upon all in the room that she was *very* important, and that Doc was running late to see her little white Bichon Frise whose name was proudly displayed on the cage: "Sire." Sire's little face peaked through the cage door—two black eyes and a black nose on white fur—looking a bit like frosty the snowman doing time.

From a warn, wooden side table, I grabbed a copy of *Sports Illustrated* and found an article on Walter Payton. Halfway through reading it, Sire and his master got called in for their turn. Sire kept yapping away, and I hoped that whatever procedure he was at the clinic for included immediate sedation just to squelch his bark which was beginning to feel like the Chinese water torture on my brain. A little later, Cathy's head popped up and peered over the counter and said, "Michael, go on in and introduce yourself to Doc while he finishes with his last patients for the day." The story on Sweetness would have to wait, and I wasn't concentrating on the article much anyway with Sire's bark echoing through the lobby from the exam room.

I stood up and walked through a set of swinging white shutter doors split down the middle, sort of like those you might see in a saloon in the Wild West, and entered the exam area where Doc held Sire in one arm like a running back holds a football, with the palm of his other hand flush against Sire's ass. As I greeted him hello he pulled his index finger out of the dog, a single brown digit covered in feces, which he then held in the air to wave at me while smiling and raising his eyebrows high over his spectacles.

"Hunkey dorey. Everything's fine with this one! He is officially *un-plugged.* You must be Michael," he smiled, but only after noticing the rubber glove over his soiled finger could I break from the distraction and muster a response.

"Uh, yes sir. Actually, everyone calls me Mike. Either is fine though. Jeff says you are looking for another kennel boy, I mean vet assistant," I said. Attempting not to be too obvious in avoiding his handshake, I nonchalantly slipped my hands into my jean pockets.

"Mrs. Cartwright, Sire is just fine. He was a bit backed up, and I pulled some foil out which suggests he got into your candy jar again. Remember, chocolate and other sweets are not good for these little guys. Just some boiled rice and water for him until tomorrow, then back to dry dog food and no people food. See you next time."

Dr. Dodson walked toward the sink and pulled the latex glove off his right hand, then grabbed a nearby bar of Ivory soap and vigorously washed his hands. Other than the many white Formica cabinets that lined the walls of the room, a floor-level scale for weighing dogs and cats, and a small makeshift fish tank atop a metal file cabinet containing a pet tarantula, the most noticeable item in the exam room was a nicely framed diploma hanging above the sink: "Robert David Dodson, Doctor of Veterinary Medicine, University of Illinois."

I realized my palms were sweaty, though I hadn't anticipated being nervous applying for a job which I assumed would primarily consist of discarding dog and cat droppings from cages and sweeping and mopping the floors.

"People call me Doc, which you can call me too. Jeff says you and he go to the same church and the same high school, and that your dad is a policeman in Dolton. As you know, Jeff is graduating soon then leaving for college, so I need someone to learn the job and take over for him. I only ask that you are on time, listen to what you're told and work hard. I have a few other kids who have inquired about the job, but if you want it, it's yours."

"Yes. Absolutely. I'm very interested. Thanks Dr. Dodson, I mean, Doc." He extended his freshly washed hand and shook mine. The picture of his shit-covered finger, even under a layer of thin rubber, still flashed in my mind as we shook hands. Doc's large, meaty hand extended from a somewhat imposing figure. Doc and his exam room reminded me a bit of a Norman Rockwell photo I once saw in the *Saturday Evening Post* entitled "Before the Shot," showing a little boy in a doctor's office pulling down his trousers for a vaccination while reading the doctor's diploma on the wall. A grandfatherly type, the round spectacles that sat squarely on the end of Doc's nose and his broad smile gave way to a soft, gentle presence who I imagined most people trusted implicitly with their beloved dogs and cats. Doc was around 60, easily six foot three and 240 pounds, a little pudgy around the middle, with large, clunky feet that echoed throughout the clinic every time he moved. Mostly though, he described the job as one of importance, with responsibilities beyond the sort of stuff I was used to. But I also had the impression he would be a good guy to work for, and I felt in the moment I had lucked out with my new gig.

Jeff trained me for several weeks, showing me around the clinic as I tapped into his knowledge about how to help Doc restrain ornery dogs during examination, how to assist during surgeries, and how to clean the basement pens without being bitten by dogs or scratched by cats.

While in the basement pen area, Jeff pulled a step stool from a closet, looked around to make sure no one was coming, and popped up one of the ceiling tiles and reached around for something above. He pulled out the most bizarre item I had ever seen, a necklace made from discarded puppy tails, trimmed puppy ears and dew claws. It smelled a bit, but was unlike anything I had ever seen. Black, brown, tan and white tails and flaps of puppy ears, still soft and furry and mostly less than four inches, some with spotted tips, alternated between crescent-shaped dew claws which clanked together like an out of tune wind chime as he dangled the necklace. Each dog part was sewn together with a thick thread and then knotted so it could be worn as a necklace.

"Isn't this cool? It's been passed on by each group of kids who worked here. Some girl named Joy started it around seven years ago. See any time Doc clips puppy tails or ears, or removes dew claws, we secretly pull them out of the trash. Then after everyone has gone home we add them on to this necklace. Want to try it on?"

"Nah. Looks pretty neat though. What do you do with it?" I asked. It reminded me of something an Indian chief might wear at tribal meetings to ward off evil spirits.

"Nothing really. But when Doc's wife Nancy comes around to mess with us you'll wish you could use it to cast a spell on her!"

Jeff put the necklace back, and I wondered what he meant about Mrs. Dodson.

Doc's house was connected to the clinic by a single hallway on the main level. The clinic itself was not large—front lobby with Cathy's desk behind a tall counter and around a dozen blue plastic chairs and a table for magazines, a center examination area including a wooden exam table and some basic supplies, and a small back room where the surgeries were conducted. Before exiting from the rear of the clinic was Doc's small office, which contained a desk, an old wooden chair on wheels (looked like the one Barney Fife used to sit on) and several bookshelves, all of which held piles and piles of books, papers, files, and boxes filled with more papers and files. At the very back of the clinic beyond a small hallway was an unfinished room called the "holding room" with a gray concrete floor containing three large chain link cages and a door to the back yard. Doc let the kennel kids sign their names on the wall of the holding room before they left for college. A stairwell from the holding room led down to the basement "pen room" of the clinic, where a large wall of different sized stainless steel animal pens held dogs and cats waiting to be picked up by their owners or that were scheduled for exams and surgeries the following day. Stray dogs and cats were dropped off from time to time by neighbors or the police or animal control. They were held in the pen room for ten days, after which—if unclaimed or not adopted—they were euthanized.

"The coolest part of this job is in the summer you get extra hours to do yard work and sometimes Doc lets you use his riding mower," Jeff said as he put fresh newspaper in one of the pens. "But you really gotta watch out for Doc's wife. She is pure evil. I mean, really one nasty bitch."

This statement caught my attention, given the urgency with which Jeff emphasized his description of Mrs. Dodson. Though any words of wisdom as the new guy were helpful, this advice seemed a bit late if not moot. Like getting on an airplane and being told after takeoff that it's desperately due for an oil change and low on gas.

Jeff proceeded to tell me his version of Mrs. Dodson, a retired English teacher whose students always hated her and played mean tricks on her, now with too much time on her hands and only the job of caretaking for her 85 year-old, senile mother to occupy her. Apparently she was never able to have kids, another source of tension in her life, and she appeared to have little use for Doc's puttering around the house after work, or spending hours on end each weekend out in the garden.

"Just stay out of her way, and always try to look busy when she's around. If she catches you not working, she will pull you aside and have you doing chores in her house, like washing the windows using newspaper, or spraying her attic with bleach, or some other bullshit," Jeff said as he briskly moved back and forth between the pens and the sink, filling bowls with water and food. The old, white cast iron sink in the pen room reminded me of the one in my grandma's laundry room. Because the basement pen room of the clinic adjoined the laundry room of Doc's home connected by a door with a large, square glass window at the top, I got busy and began helping Jeff with the pens. With the light on in the pen room and the light off in the adjoining laundry room, I could never tell whether I was being watched by Doc's wife or not, which made the pen room a bit spooky.

The first weeks and months at SHACK were exciting, mostly because I felt like helping to fix whatever the dogs and cats were brought in for was a real contribution, like I was actually doing some good through my work. During the second week there I helped Doc deliver a litter of kittens, which—although gross at the time— was actually pretty fascinating.

When my friends at school found out I worked for a vet they were intrigued and asked lots of questions. Have you ever been bitten? What kinds of animals do you see there? Does he really have a pet tarantula? Are you going to be a veterinarian when you grow up? I became very knowledgeable on all things four-legged, and my cool quotient at school tripled.

Though I was nonchalant about accepting the job initially, over time I got in to working at the SHACK. Doc took immense pride in his work, booked as many appointments each day that he could squeeze in, and his customers always seemed happy because their little dogs and cats left in better shape than they arrived in. I got to learn the different dog and cat breeds, the differences in their behavior and temperament, the proper diagnosis and medicine to treat them, and how to connect with animals to gain their trust. Looking back, I'm fairly certain my current work ethic is attributable to working for Doc.

Before long the kids at school couldn't wait to hear of my animal clinic exploits at lunch each day. They most loved my description of how Doc performed the cat neuters. One slit of the scalpel on the skin of each testicle sack, then a pull of the testicle and spermatic cord was all it took. Then Doc dangled the cat's balls like fuzzy dice until they lightly touched the cat's lips and he would say, "Kiss them goodbye," before hurling them into the slop bucket. Definitely the easiest $90 a vet could make in only five minutes.

By July, Jeff was off to Illinois State University and I was now "senior kennel boy" on a staff of one. But I could tell Doc sort of took to me, calling me Michael even though I mentioned a few times most of my friends called me Mike. It was obvious that although Doc never had kids, he treated the kennel kids much like his own, invested in teaching them and making them laugh.

I learned that Doc was in the Navy, and he recounted lots of funny stories about his days in the service. How he gave his sergeants "sir sandwiches," starting and ending every sentence with sir. How he and Nancy met at their high school spring dance, and how she supported him with her teacher's job while he finished veterinary school.

As easy as it was to get to know Doc and Cathy, I couldn't warm to Mrs. Dodson. I once accidentally called her Nancy, which drew a brow furrowing scowl from her, suggesting this was way too informal. I was to strictly call her Mrs. Dodson. Since I made a point to keep busy in her presence, I hadn't yet gotten pulled into her lair for any personal house chores. Sometimes at the end of the day, Cathy and I would chat while she prepared to deposit the day's income and I swept and mopped the floors. As Jeff had told me earlier, Cathy revealed to me that Doc and Nancy tried for years to have children but that Nancy's body "couldn't accommodate kids." I thought this was a strange way to put it, but I understood it to mean she had some sort of biological defect. I gathered that somehow this was told to me by Cathy to perhaps mitigate any ill will I might feel toward Nancy for being nasty all the time. That perhaps I would feel sorry for her and give her a pass. Nancy was much nicer to Cathy than she was to me and Jeff, probably because she knew Cathy was underpaid and overworked, but Cathy also saw how Nancy mistreated the kennel kids. I assumed Doc was also disappointed by not being able to have kids, and by comparison he was much nicer than his chilly wife.

One morning a beautiful Golden Retriever was dropped off. Cathy asked me to take her from her owner in the lobby and bring her downstairs and place her in a pen until her surgery later that day. I greeted her owner—a middle-aged man who looked like a construction worker of some sort—and took the leash from him to lead her away. Her thick red collar adorned her name in tiny rhinestones- LADY.

"Be nice to everyone, girl. See you this afternoon," her owner called out looking after us as I led Lady behind Cathy's desk and out of the lobby. I could tell by the way the man looked at Lady as I escorted her away that she meant a great deal to him.

Lady wagged her tail as I led her through the clinic, and I immediately noticed her limp. I pet her on the head a bit as Doc taught me so she could accept my scent, and she licked my hand and panted a bit as we headed toward the back stairs and down into the pen room. I clipped her patient card to the front of her cage and read that she was scheduled for surgery to repair a leg that had been damaged when she was hit by a car. Seems Doc had already repaired the leg once, but it needed a tune-up. I remembered being told not to give the pre-surgery animals any food or water, though her tongue hung out and she panted rapidly looking like she was incredibly thirsty.

"Sorry girl. You'll have to wait until Doc fixes you up. No water for now," I said to Lady as I cleaned the other pens. Afterward I headed outside to do yard work, and around an hour lady Cathy waved me inside.

"Michael, Doc wants you to help him in surgery this morning. He's ready for you to bring Lady up."

I headed inside, washed up, and went down to retrieve her. Her panting had slowed, and she was on her side resting. As I approached her cage she popped up and began panting heavily again and wagging her tail. She really seemed to love people, and I felt connected to her for no particular reason. She just seemed more friendly and lovable than many of the other dogs I had met up to that point.

I removed Lady from her pen, tethered a leash to her collar and led her upstairs and out the rear door into the back yard. Animals heading to surgery were always to be let out one more time to reduce the added mess of urinating or defecating on the surgery table after being anesthetized.

"Come on girl, do your thing." Lady hobbled through the back door jerking the leash along with me into the yard, and squatted down on a patch of grass to pee. Her head turned back toward me checking to make sure I was still with her. Though she was an older dog, she had a youthful energy, and I could tell she wanted to play outside for a while before heading back in. I would have liked throwing a ball and running around with her for a bit, but Doc was waiting.

"Good girl. Alright, let's go see the Doc. He'll fix you right up." I gave her a solid pat on the back of her neck and she nuzzled my arm with her snout. Lady seemed like a great family pet, one I would bring home if she were abandoned and beg my parents to let me keep.

We cut through the back holding area and emerged into the surgery room. Like most other rooms in the clinic, the surgery room smelled of alcohol and bleach. I got to know the mix of these competing smells very well while at SHACK. We used a watered down alcohol solution on the animals before injections or incisions, and a watered down bleach solution to spray the stainless steel exam tables and counter tops. Then, at the end of the day, my final chore was to sweep and bleach mop the entire clinic.

Of all the rooms in the clinic, the surgery room was my favorite. In it was a long stainless steel table with lots of handles and gadgets underneath. A hole at the end of the table that drained any liquids into a large steel bucket hanging from one end was the table's centerpiece, set below a large bright spotlight on a chain hanging from the ceiling. Oak cabinets with glass doors exposed vials of medicine, pill bottles, boxes, and other supplies over a smooth white countertop with a large steel sink. Along the counter were shiny instruments used for surgeries, glass jars with silver lids with gumball-shaped handles containing cotton balls, gauze, syringes, and long QTips, much like a regular doctor's office. An autoclave used to sterilize the surgical instruments and that looked a bit like a miniature torpedo occupied much of the counter space next to the sink. Since I had already been trained on how to sterilize the tools for surgery, Doc trusted me to help with the various operations he conducted. This was my favorite part of the job, and I think Doc enjoyed the companionship during surgeries and the opportunity to tell stories.

"Thanks for bringing her outside first. It always helps reduce the urine they release after I put them under," Doc said as he tilted the table at a slight angle toward the end holding the bucket. Doc sometimes repeated himself, but I didn't mind. He told some of the same stories over and over: when he got caught with the captain's daughter at an officer's dance at the Naval base, when he forgot to close up an animal he had operated on in vet school, and when, on the first day he opened SHACK, he slipped on some dog shit he didn't see on the floor and landed in it.

We lifted Lady onto the table, and Doc wrapped a tourniquet around her front paw after affectionately rubbing behind her ears. Animals took to Doc like they spoke the same language. I handed Doc the clippers so he could shave a spot on her front leg to insert the anesthesia. As he clicked on the clippers, the light above the surgery table flickered for a second. It reminded me a little of the lab in the old Frankenstein movie. One push of the syringe into the vein just above her front paw and Lady reclined onto her side and fell into a deep slumber. I pulled her tongue aside as Doc had trained me, and he inserted a long, crescent shaped tube down her throat, and fired up the oxygen machine.

"There you go, Ms. Lady. Now our patient won't feel a thing," Doc said to Lady, or me, or perhaps both. It took me a bit to get used to referring to animals as patients. Doc indicated that Lady required a rear leg amputation. I washed my hands, unpacked the instrument tray and set it in front of him on the surgery table.

"So how's your summer going, Michael?" Doc asked while pulling a rubber glove over each hand and scooting his chair up to the table. "Kick up the O_2 on the tank a bit, will you?" I reached over and increased the oxygen level on the large green tank a quarter turn, until Doc winked at me to stop, and then pulled up the other tiny chair on swiveling wheels and prepared to hand Doc the instruments he requested. Usually he grabbed them himself, and I handed him gauze to blot the bleeding.

"Fine. It's nice sleeping in a bit and not having homework or wrestling practice," I replied.

Doc quickly shaved Lady's rear right leg down to the skin in the area he intended to cut. As the fur flew off Lady it occurred to me they were the exact same clippers that my barber used on me at the Dolton Snip-n-Clip when I was a kid. Had I known that barbers and vets had so much in common, I might not have felt so special when Dad took me for my buzz cuts. Lady looked strange missing all her fur on one hind quarter though.

"Two years ago I put a metal connecting plate in her leg after she was hit by a car. I recommended they let me amputate it then, but they preferred to shell out the money for a special plate so she could partially use it. But now the bone has splintered further and she isn't using the leg much at all, so we need to remove the leg from around the knee down before it becomes infected. Have you ever seen a three-legged dog? They're actually pretty mobile."

I had already helped him with some spays and neuters, so the sight of blood and seeing him make incisions through animal flesh with a scalpel was no problem. But the thought of a three-legged dog, which I had *not* ever seen before, had me somewhat distracted.

"Gauze, Michael. Keep up as you see it getting heavier," Doc instructed. "Actually, once I get the leg off I need you to take it to the sink and cut the stainless steel plate out. They're expensive, and I can sanitize it and reuse it on another dog later. You'll need the surgical allen wrench to unscrew it."

By this time Doc had already begun cutting through Lady's flesh around the knee, using clamps to contain the small amount of bleeding. Then, without warning, he hit a major artery that erupted like a geyser and shot blood three feet above the operating table, spraying the overhead light like a fire hose while Doc scrambled for a larger clamp.

"Jiminy crickets! More gauze! Pack it and hold it while I find the source."

Like using napkins to soak up spilled ketchup at the dinner table, I greedily grabbed wads of gauze and stuffed them onto Lady's leg as it continued to spew blood. The gauze changed from white to pink to red immediately. Then Doc found the severed artery and with one click of a clamp had it contained.

"That could have been a disaster," Doc said as he grabbed clean gauze to wipe his blood-sprayed glasses. Cathy heard the commotion and came in, handing Doc a fresh smock and new gloves.

"Michael, go clean yourself up downstairs, and bring up the bucket and mop," Doc said. I headed downstairs and quickly retrieved the bucket, filled it with bleach water and rushed back upstairs.

By the time I returned Cathy had cleaned up most of the blood, except on the light above which would be cleaned after we were done and it had time to cool. For now it steamed a bit from the red liquid bubbling on the large, orb-like bulb. I mopped up the remaining blood under the table, then sat back down to help Doc finish up. By this time Lady's leg was totally separated from her body, and she was still covered in a good amount of blood. For the first time working at SHACK, I felt a bit queasy.

As I sat back down, Mrs. Dodson entered the room. Though usually I could detect the approach of her gait by its speedy cadence and busy myself before her arrival, this time she caught me off guard. I could tell it appeared to her I was loafing.

"Robert, I have some chores I could use Michael's help with. I see he isn't too busy right now, so I'll borrow him for a bit and return him shortly." Doc didn't answer, but his non-response reinforced what Jeff once told me—like the many dogs escorted into SHACK controlled by their owners, Doc's wife held the leash. Not only with Doc, but with everyone in the clinic. Doc was the boss, but Nancy was in charge. She gestured toward me, rolling her index finger toward herself peering over her bifocals. And like the animals relenting to their masters who came through SHACK each day, I obediently cowered and followed.

"You can retrieve the plate from the leg bone when you get back. I'll leave it in the sink for you." Doc said this like it was somehow supposed to compensate for Nancy leading me away to help with her house chores. Like a kid getting ice cream for finishing his plate.

I spent the next two hours organizing gardening supplies in Mrs. Dodson's greenhouse, sweeping the garage, hosing off the front porch, and cleaning the house windows inside and out. She insisted I use newspaper when I did the windows. This saved money and did a better job, according to her. Doc told me many times that when he was growing up they used the "daily rag" for lots of household chores, and that this was a common reference to the local newspaper.

I didn't work any harder when I was in Doc's house helping Nancy with her chores, but the work just felt harder because of her relentless supervision. She hovered over me pointing out smudges I missed in the large glass sliding door. With her two large Japanese Akitas, Hercules and Kita, licking, snorting and clawing at the glass to go outside all day, the window was a never-ending project that was never quite restored to its original clarity. She repeatedly said, "Take your time and do a good job, or you'll have to start over."

There was no conversation, no interest in me as a person, just constant nudging for me to get as much done as possible in the time she had her hooks in me. And it seemed no matter how much care and attention I gave toward doing it right, it was never good enough. It had been a few years since I read Cinderella, but I was starting to identify with how she felt (and in retrospect, Nancy inadvertently taught me why micromanagement is not a model for good supervision).

I finished up and returned to the surgery room to find Lady's leg waiting for me in the sink. It looked strange sitting there motionless with no body attached to it, and for a second I was sad that she wouldn't enjoy its use any more. But I also couldn't wait to tell my friends about the three-legged dog and its fountain of blood. I used a scalpel to cut through the leg muscle until I hit bone, and then cut along the bone until I felt the razor snag on something hard. I could tell I hit metal, and cut toward it until I could see the plate, still bright silver, connected to the bone with three tiny screws. Unlike fixing the chain on my bike or using a screwdriver to help Dad, this felt different, more important. This wasn't sweeping the floors or toiling over Nancy's windows, this was more precise. Holding a scalpel like Doc made me feel he had confidence and trust in me to do it right, the counter opposite to how I felt moments earlier hovering beneath his wife as she pointed out my imperfections.

I removed the plate, cleaned it, and then scrubbed all the surgical instruments before placing them back in their tray and inserting the tray into the autoclave. I sprayed the table with bleach water and wiped it town, turned off the light so I could circle back and wipe the blood off the bulb after it cooled, and headed to the basement to clean the pens and prepare for the day-end sweeping and mopping. I was eager to check on Lady to see if she was awake from surgery yet.

I made my way downstairs and swung open the door to the usual meows and barks prompted by my entry to the pen room each time. In my mind it was akin to the applause someone very important experienced when they stepped on stage. Often just to make Jeff laugh I would enter the pen room and graciously bow to the yapping animals, then in my best Elvis voice would say, "Thank you. Thank you very much." I flipped on the fluorescent lights and they flickered a bit before illuminating a sight I was not expecting: Lady's teeth clamped tight on the bars of her cage door, eyes wide open but motionless, rigor mortis already beginning to take hold. I knew before moving closer that she was gone. My chest began to rise, and as I exhaled the tears began to stream down my cheeks.

I realized, after working there a few months, that death regularly visited the SHACK. Doc euthanized a few dogs and cats each week. Some of old age, some who were too sick to live, some having been hit by cars or attacked by other animals. After a while it didn't faze me to linger as a dog's owner wept profusely while saying final goodbyes. After their car exited the parking lot, I would scoop the dead animal into a black trash bag and throw it over my shoulder like Santa Claus, carry it to Doc's garage, then heave it into the large white freezer. This task became second nature, other than the time I used both hands and, like an Olympian doing the hammer throw, swung too hard and a heavy German Sheppard broke through the bottom of the bag and flew across Doc's garage floor and under his Lincoln Continental.

But the longer I worked there, the stranger things got. On more than a few occasions I would finish sweeping and mopping the entire clinic, carry the mop and bucket downstairs into the basement, and emerge back to the main level only to find tracks of muddy shoe prints across the floor, requiring me to mop all over again. These shoe prints were always the same size and shape as Mrs. Dodson's. Typically she came in late to drag the oxygen tank into her bedroom to help her sleep at night. Cathy said she suffered from "chronic migraines." I was pretty sure it was nothing other than a volatile mix of mid-life crisis with a smattering of menopause and a dollop of hemorrhoids. All told, enough to make even the most cantankerous woman purely wicked.

After a while the initial intrigue of the job wore off and it was just like most other jobs, something that brought in some cash and, mostly, kept me out of trouble. Before Jeff left for college he let me in on a few secrets. Where Doc's liquor cabinet was, where his wife kept her stash of European chocolates, and where Doc kept the spare keys to his Lincoln. He also showed me how to deal with any of the problem animals.

Jeff kept a spare wooden broom handle under the sink in the basement, along with an L-shaped nail which fit perfectly into a hole at the end of the broom stick. He showed me how to use a leash to create a noose with the stick, so that if I couldn't get a cat out of its cage without being hissed at, sprayed or bitten, the noose could be used to subdue the animal until it calmed down enough to be grabbed behind the neck and lifted from a dirty cage to a clean one. Cruel as this sounds, as long as the proper amount of pressure was applied to the noose—restricting the animal's air intake but not cutting off its breathing—it worked like a charm. Plus it was better than being scratched or bitten, which was a daily hazard in the pen area.

Most of the time this little trick worked well, and the meanest, nastiest cats could be dealt with accordingly. Other than Cathy coming down occasionally to check on things, I was the only one in the basement pen room taking care of the animals.

One afternoon I reached in to pull a Tabby cat from her cage, and I must have startled her from her sleep. She lunged at my arm, bit down and then scratched my hand in a flash of fury.

"Damn! You little shit!"

She recoiled to the corner of the pen and reared up like a cornered boxer, hissing loudly and preparing for a second strike. I retrieved the broom handle, inserted the nail and hooked up the noose, and within a few tries had it snug around the Tabby's neck. She lunged toward me and while her momentum brought her toward the cage door I swung her into the air hovering just above the floor until her legs stuck straight out and her eyes bulged from her nasty little head. As I lowered her to the floor to recover, Mrs. Dodson came roaring through the door, emerging from the darkened laundry room with a basket full of clothes in her hands.

"How dare you! You have no right to treat an animal that way. This will be your last day working here, that's for sure. I'll see to it!" She dropped the basket of laundry and stomped up the stairs into the clinic. I knew I was pinched, and thought for sure I would be fired. As I picked up the cat and placed her into a clean pen, she came to looking like a groggy sailor awakening after a night of heavy drinking. I heard Doc's heavy footsteps coming down the stairs and toward the pen door. Nancy was nowhere to be seen.

"I see you picked up on Jeff's little system. Truth is, I taught him how to do it, but only to control the animal and prevent injury. If you pull a cat from the cage and let her hang, you'll either snap her neck or cut off her wind and suffocate her, and in either case I will be in a heap of trouble," Doc said. I was embarrassed, but relieved he wasn't angrier. He was talking just above a whisper, and then said in an even lower voice, "Now I've got to give you the business a bit since Mrs. Dodson is at the top of the stairs listening down. Don't worry, you're not going to lose your job. We'll talk more about it later—" and in a raised tone and angry voice, led straight to his next statement, just for effect… "Are you out of your mind?! Do you have any idea what could have happened? I have half a mind to have you call this poor cat's owner and describe what you did to it. Get back to work before I really lose my cool!" Doc yelled and then, with a wink, turned and stomped back up the stairs. As relieved as I was not to be fired, I paused to think about how bad I would feel to tell the cat's owner that I hung it into submission. I decided to leave the mop handle trick alone for a while.

By my senior year in high school, I was working four afternoons a week at SHACK, plus weekends in the summer, and—like Jeff before me—was asked to find a replacement before I left for college. My friend Jay—who unlike me actually did want to be a vet—wanted the job, so I put in a good word for him with Doc. Doc hired him and asked me to train him before leaving for college.

By June I only had a few weeks left and my relationship with Doc had developed into a trusting friendship. He asked me to come by the clinic a few extra times over the upcoming weekend to take care of Hercules and Kita while he and Mrs. Dodson were out of town on a trip. I mentioned this to a few friends, and before I knew it word spread that I was hosting a party at the SHACK. I figured this would be a great way to end my senior year, so I told a few people to stop by the clinic Friday night around eight. Jay and I arrived early and made sure Doc's basement bar was stocked.

About a dozen friends arrived, and I felt pretty cool welcoming them to a huge house with a nice finished basement that contained a bar and pool table. Things were mellow until about nine, when there were closer to twenty-five kids there and we had located Doc's stereo and cranked the tunes.

"Walks, we need to make a beer run," a guy named Scott said.

"Go out the side door quietly, and make sure you park around back again when you return." Scott and a guy I barely knew named Danny took up a collection for beer and headed for Tom's Liquors, a few miles from SHACK in nearby Harvey.

I returned to drinking beer with a few friends until I realized Scott and Danny had been gone nearly an hour. I left the basement to cut through the laundry room toward the pen room, and heard noise and whispering in the clinic. I made my way upstairs and rounded the corner to find Scott and Danny rummaging through the medicine cabinets in the darkened surgery room, using only a small flashlight.

"What the hell are you guys doing up here? I thought you were making a beer run?" I asked, agitated.

"Dude. We're just checking things out. I've never been in an animal hospital. Pretty cool," Scott replied. Danny was shifting something in the front pocket of his hooded sweatshirt, and looked really suspicious. He closed a cabinet door and attempted to head past me.

"What's in your pocket?" I asked.

Danny replied, "You don't want to know, and you don't need to know. Just forget we were even up here and everything will be cool." I decided it would be better to diffuse the situation than risk a fight and brawling in the clinic, so I followed them out to their car as they left.

When I arrived back in the basement I reminded everyone to stay downstairs and to be cool, that we would all be busted if anyone discovered we were there. Other than a few spilled drinks and some girl who threw up in Doc's toilet, the rest of the night went off okay and Doc never uttered a word of suspicion about what happened.

Sitting in homeroom the last day of my senior year, I noticed several police cars pulling up to the front of the school. This was fairly routine, given the number of students who were enrolled and the trouble they got into. But when, shortly thereafter, I saw Scott and Danny being escorted into a squad car in handcuffs, my heart sank.

"Man, did you hear about what happened to Scott and Danny?" Jay rushed up to me and asked as I exited class. I shook my head no.

"They were trying to sell a few vials of some sort of steroid to some football players and got caught. They're going straight to jail right now."

The following day's local *South Suburban News* headlines read, "Two Dolton youths arrested for peddling Equipoise." The article indicated that Equipoise is an expensive horse hormone that, when taken in smaller doses, doubles as an anabolic steroid popular among professional athletes.

As far as I could tell from the article, they hadn't yet rolled over and told where they got it from. But Doc had been good to me, taken care of me for two years, given me a few raises, and talked to me about stuff that was on my mind, and even protected my job when Nancy wanted me fired. I felt downright guilty about hosting the party. I doubted I could head off to college with this weighing on my conscience, so on my last day of work I asked Doc if we could go to lunch together. He gladly obliged with his usual phrase: "Only if you let me buy."

At lunch I got up the nerve to tell Doc about the party, and about the theft that occurred. He looked really surprised at first, and then said, "Well I admire you for being honest, and I will need to let the police know where they got it from. I don't get many calls to treat horses much anymore, so it would have been months before I noticed it was missing. But I'm glad they were apprehended before anyone used the stuff. It's not meant for human beings and could be dangerous to mess with."

I was sad to say goodbye to Doc as I left that day, and embarrassed that I had left an otherwise great experience on such a low note. Scott and Danny never implicated me in the theft and said I had no knowledge they took the Equipoise, which was basically true.

Several months after beginning college my mom called to tell me she read in the obituaries that Dr. Robert Dodson died in his sleep of a heart attack at the age of 63, a decorated Naval veteran of the Korean War with no children and survived by his wife of 42 years. The next time I was back in town I drove to the SHACK only to find it lifeless and abandoned, waist high grass and weeds covering the lawn I once took pride in mowing, and adorning a For Sale sign. My curiosity motivated me toward closer inspection, so I parked the car and walked around a bit.

Most of the windows were boarded up, except the windows in back outside the holding room. I peered in expecting to see a roomful of barking dogs, and the usual images of the bustling South Holland Animal Clinic staff—Cathy bringing dogs and cats in and out, the kennel kids hustling around to help, and Doc smiling and laughing at his own jokes while treating another customer's beloved pet.

But I blinked and the holding room was dark and desolate. Devoid of life, human or animal. The kennel kids' names inscribed on the wall showed the history of those who had been part of the SHACK. Other than the pen fences, two other items in the room caught my eye. A red dog collar with the name LADY hung from a nail high on the wall, above the letters RIP in my handwriting. And on a nearby nail hung the voodoo necklace once hidden in the pen room, above a signature that read, "To the SHACK kennel kids. Love, Doc."

THEN THERE WAS THE SAV

I was six or seven, and we were sitting around a campfire with some families we met at the campground while on vacation. Mom was relaxed, wearing shorts, smoking a cigarette and drinking a beer. A little girl from another campsite was next to me, roasting a marshmallow on the end of a stick. Typical for little kids cooking marshmallows on sticks, she would let the mallow catch fire, blow it out, let its black ashes cool, then devour it. After eating a few, she decided to try a new technique to extinguish her mallow. She stuck one on the end of the stick, placed it deep into the hot embers of the fire, then pulled the little ball of flame out and began furiously waving the stick back and forth to try to extinguish it using the force of the night air against the enflamed fireball. Like a rubber pencil, after a few waves of the stick the flaming marshmallow flew off like a gooey meteor, landed on my Mom's exposed thigh, and sent her screaming back toward our tent. The flaming marshmallow incident is a metaphor for my Mom's life. Every time she permitted herself to relax, without warning a meteor struck. She never saw any of it coming, and each one burned as hot as the last.

The examples were many. Woken from a deep sleep to rush my brother Todd to the hospital during another asthma attack when he was two. Playing with us in the back yard when two pretty young women stopped by on their bikes asking if my Dad was around because they needed to discuss "police business." Waking up to hear Dad talking in his sleep about another woman. Managing four boys on her own after my Dad moved out, then taking him back in a year later. A call from her sister-in-law that her brother Bob had died suddenly of a heart attack at forty-two, followed by a call the next year that her other brother Gil died suddenly of a heart attack at forty-four. Getting ready for Christmas Eve church service only to answer a knock at the door to find a strange eighteen-year-old girl holding a newborn baby, claiming it was my brother Dave's kid, turning Mom instantly into an unknowing grandmother at 43. And years later getting settled in a beautiful little house after her divorce, then being diagnosed with Pancreatic cancer.

Mom's life was a string of surprise attacks, but she remained the optimistic matriarch of our family. Family picnics, reunions, holiday gatherings, paper drives, church functions. She orchestrated it all with consummate ease and finesse, never letting life's little surprises break her spirit. And she did it raising four boys whose combined energy and mishaps were enough to put anyone in the funny farm.

She lost track of the number of times David was sent home from school for disrespecting teachers. She answered countless knocks at the door from neighbors complaining David and I trashed their houses during Halloween vandalism sprees. Todd's emotional, middle child outbursts and repeated doctor's visits. Then the arrival of a fourth son, Dennis, after it appeared Mom and Dad were done raising kids. Four boys and two dogs bounding about in a small two-level, three bedroom home in little town, U.S.A. Four boys eating Mom and Dad out of house and home, on a tight budget. Utter chaos most days. Enough to drive a Mom to drink, a lot.

Mom's mom, Grandma Gerritsen, had ten sisters and a brother, all of whom settled in the south suburbs of Chicago, and my Mom was the glue that held the entire clan together. She hosted family picnics for hundreds of relatives. Every week she arranged a rotating pinnacle card party at each family's house in order to help keep the family ties strong. Grandma Gerritsen didn't drive, so she and her sister Dolores picked up her groceries, did her yard work, and drove her to church every week. Mom organized it all like a cruise director. Everyone loved Aunt Betty, and Aunt Betty took care of everyone. She loved her boys, and loved our Dad.

Dad was a good provider and workaholic, but—like most other Doltonites—wasn't a big advocate of the Golden Rule. Whether Dad's conservative attitude was a function of being a cop, or as a cop he just learned to sound hateful to fit in with the other cops, I'm not sure. But Dad was a generous and likable guy, went out of his way to help others, and worked tirelessly to provide for his family. He pulled extra shifts as a cop and did odd jobs such as landscaping on weekends just to help make ends meet. But he had this intolerable habit of watching the evening news while we ate dinner and editorialized every segment. Sort of like having Rush Limbaugh over for supper every night.

"Let's see what disruption black people are causing the City of Chicago today."

"I see the Chicago school system is about to discriminate against white teachers by using a quota system to hire minority applicants."

"Can you believe we are about to hire black police officers? Next we'll be hiring females as well!"

These were among his more common responses as WGN aired the Chicago news, and—though not intended as such—this was our nightly lesson in hate. He didn't look much like Archie Bunker—no cigar and no recliner—but they definitely coached from the same playbook. It was too late for him and most of his generation to un-learn their hate. Hatred learned from their parents and the absence of higher education to mollify its effects rendered my Dad and my friends' parents representative of a generation of mistrusting and suspicious people.

Not to generalize, because many great and open-minded Americans were also born of the post-WWII generation, but most whites in Chicago's south suburbs when I grew up had no tolerance for diversity. I don't remember ever hearing an adult say, "Treat everyone with dignity and respect." "Color doesn't matter." "Learn from people different from you." Instead, it was a racially charged environment which, in many ways, has yet to change.

While Dad may have never benefited from formal education, and all the racial bias and stereotypes he engendered were taught to him by his parents' generation, he was otherwise a great father. As a kid I didn't notice his indifference to people of color, so I didn't pay much attention to it. I only saw him there for us, providing for us, and giving us the basic things kids sought—a swing set in the yard, bicycles, a backyard clubhouse to play in, mini-bikes, an above-ground swimming pool, access to a lake for swimming and fishing. He and Mom loved their kids and spent every day trying to make us happy. Like most families, there was laughter and there were tears, but love permeated it all.

Dad always made sure we were involved in little league sports. He coached our football teams year after year, even after working double shifts. He set aside enough money for annual summer vacations and one trip to Disney World (with another cop's family which also had four boys...stuffing eight kids and four adults in a Winnebago from Chicago down to Orlando was enough to put any parent over the edge).

Though my parents emphasized the general importance of school, there wasn't a check and balance system to really instill in me the critical need for education early on. Mom and Dad were somewhat indifferent to grades, as long as my brothers and I passed and would graduate. Other than focusing on the sport of wrestling, the rest of my time was spent drinking beer and practicing drums with my band Sinjiin. Every week was the same: school, work at various after-school clean-up jobs, then partying on Friday and Saturday nights. As a sophomore I began dating one of the smartest girls in school who was undoubtedly college-bound (cheerleader, editor of the school newspaper, really had her act together and got a scholarship to Eastern Illinois University). This was a turning point for my future, and she motivated me to get it together. I went from being a C student to an A-B student, and studied hard enough to get accepted to Western Illinois University on a music scholarship. Then my sophomore year in college I met the love of my life.

Drop dead gorgeous and the life of the party, Barbie Eisenhauer grew up in upscale Sudbury, Massachusetts. Divorced parents, a family history of alcoholism, and four older, wild sisters gave us enough in common to compare notes on. By senior year in high school she needed to get out of her hometown, and abruptly moved in with her father in Prospect Heights, Illinois. No wonder when we first met I noticed her habit of pinching or "clicking" the sheets as she tried to go to sleep at night. This was a habit formed years earlier as a little kid, likely to comfort her as she tried to fall asleep while her parents went at it. We were more like best friends and drinking buddies initially. We first met as we jockeyed for position around the keg at the TKE fraternity house at WIU, and most people mistook us for brother and sister.

I knew Barb was the one I would spend the rest of my life with when my parents came to see me in the WIU marching band my sophomore year and I told them my new girlfriend would be there and I wanted them to meet. As I banged away on my drum on the fifty yard line at half time, and without ever seeing Barb or having any idea what she looked like, my Mom scanned the student section of the bleachers, picked Barb out of the crowd of thousands of other college kids, and approached her and introduced herself. "You must be Barbie." It sort of freaked Barb out, but it confirmed what we already knew—we were meant for each other.

Later that semester Barb and I returned home for the holiday break. Groggy from a late night at Romar's Tap, Barb woke to the sound of her car being started in my parents' driveway.

"Who's in my car?"

"My dad. He needs to move it out of the driveway in order to pull the van out," I said, sipping coffee while standing over her, admiring her dark skin and beautiful jet black hair.

"Shit! Steve was in my car last night, and I think he left his pipe on the gear shift console!" she sprang out of bed in one motion.

"Be cool. He knows we don't get high, and I doubt he cares if Steve does."

"But I don't want him to think *I* do," Barbie popped up and pulled her shorts on.

I headed to the kitchen prepared to present my best defense to Dad when he came back in from moving Barb's car. I took a seat at the table, nursing my hangover and coaxing each sip of coffee down. Having friends that partied wasn't the end of the world, right? Then the door opened and Dad walked in, grabbed his keys and said, "I'm heading out to run some errands. See you all later."

Assuming perhaps Barbie was mistaken about what was left in plain view in the car, I waited for him to depart and then scurried out to the front curb where he had moved her car. There it was, right in plain view. Steve's ceramic, guitar-shaped bowl. So close to the gear shifter that he would have nearly touched it when he released the parking break. And he definitely knew what a bowl looked like, having routinely confiscated them from Dolton hoodlums. Nothing. Not a word then or ever. Speaking about it would mean confrontation. Confrontation would mean dealing with it or, worse, acknowledging that his boys partied too much or kept bad company. Much easier to just let it slide.

Whether it was our reckless behavior with girls, booze or juvenile delinquency, my parents were not interested in holding us accountable. Strangely enough, Barb's dad Ron was completely different.

A wine connoisseur, Ron (an executive of Digital Equipment Corporation and who went by the name "Ike") had no tolerance for our nonsense. He traveled on business a lot, so Barb and I got to spend lots of weekends alone at his posh condo outside Chicago. One weekend when Ike was on travel we crashed there for a few nights. We decided to make a nice Italian meal together, meaning we would cook the only thing that we knew how to make at that point—spaghetti. I pulled an expensive bottle of Jordan Cabernet Sauvignon out of his private collection. Ignorant to wine etiquette, I drank half of it and then put it in the fridge. Later that night Barb and I lit his fireplace and accidentally left the flue closed, filling his living room and covering his white furniture with soot. We spent the next morning vigorously cleaning the place, convinced we had covered our tracks, then left to head back to WIU. The call from Ike to Barb when he returned from his trip wasn't pretty.

"Who drank half my expensive bottle of Jordan and ruined the rest by putting it in my refrigerator? Why is there black ash all over my god damn house? And why are there six exploded bottles of beer in my freezer!" Ike warmed to me later because he saw in me the same qualities he based his own life on—a blue collar work ethic, enjoyment of professional sports, appreciation of a good joke and having a sense of humor.

As I got to know Ike better, we accepted each other and I focused on his positive qualities. I didn't judge him because he chose his career over committing to his marriage and raising five daughters. Perhaps too much alcohol distorted his decision making. He later quit cold turkey, not an easy task for someone who drank regularly for thirty years. But Ike was always there for me and Barb when we needed him.

Having two kids, I understand that with the addition of each child in a family parents tend to become a bit battle-weary. Sometimes the first kid gets smothered with love and attention, the second kid gets a little less, and the increased age of parents and fatigue from raising each child results in gradual and increased ignorance of what each one is up to.

My brother Todd is the typical middle brother that we picked on and teased, but he got the last laugh by becoming a highly successful human resources director and two-term mayor in the bucolic suburb of Genoa, Illinois. Little brother Dennis, eight years younger than me, always viewed me as more of a second father or uncle than a brother. He looked up to me even when my friends and I tortured him as a kid: pushed him out into the middle of the lake to wade until he nearly drowned; pulled him up by his underwear, giving him atomic wedgies until he writhed in pain; hung him upside down by his ankles to retrieve a six pack from the middle of a stream; and taught him how to chug a beer at the age of fourteen during his first visit to the Teke house. What he may not know is that while he thought I was teaching him, Dennis was teaching me.

In the case of our family, it seemed as the years went by my parents were less obtrusive about what we were up to. Of course, this worked to our advantage. Our curfews got later, their supervision of us got leaner, and the fun factor increased exponentially. So my parents really had nothing left in the tank after raising their first kid—David, or as everyone referred to him as, "The Sav."

Only a year apart in age, David and I grew up together, shared a bedroom through high school, and lived together briefly in college. The Sav, short for "savage," a nickname that stuck with him from middle school through his time in the Army and beyond, was truly one of kind. Bad grades, promiscuity, drinking and smoking, and getting a girl pregnant all by the age of eighteen gave my parents all they could handle from son number one. The common boyhood hijinks that most kids were up to paled in comparison. But Sav, or Davey, as Mom and Dad always called him, had my back during many a playground brawl. Having an older brother or sister watching over you as you grow up is like a warm blanket on a cold winter night. You can live without it, but living with it is so much nicer.

David was always shorter than I, stocky, afraid of nothing and no one, and with guts atypical for kids his age. Mom said he had *Moxie*, and he tormented the neighborhood by throwing snowballs at moving cars in the winter, crabapples at cars in the summer, and on Halloween would fill paper lunch sacks with dog shit and light them on fire on neighbor's porches, ring the doorbell, and run. He once jumped through a screen door to punch a kid who pushed me around at school, and another time covered himself in shaving cream from head to toe and knocked on the door of the only Mexican family in the neighborhood and asked, "Do you have any tortilla chips for my sour cream?"

When I was in first grade we were tussling on the schoolyard during recess and he ripped my shirt. Though we were just having fun, my teacher grabbed me, dragged me to David's classroom, and made him take off his shirt in front of the whole class and switch with me. Though my teacher was trying to prove a point, David took my badly torn shirt, put it on, and smiled at her and said, "Thanks. This one fits better." It was no big deal. Not much was a big deal to Sav.

One of Sav's favorite things to do was to skeech. Skeeching is what you do in Dolton when the roads are covered in at least a few inches of snow or ice. You jump onto the back bumper of a moving car with your knees bent like a baseball catcher, and ski behind the car until it stops or you fall off. It's incredibly dangerous given that oncoming traffic can't see you kneeling behind the opposing car's bumper, and if you fall off you may tumble into the other lane. Manhole covers were also treacherous, and many kids ripped their legs wide open skeeching over dry spots in the road or stumbling over steel manhole covers. But we were fearless, and everyone was doing it. Sav was the best skeecher around.

While most kids asked siblings old enough to drive to let them grab on back of the car while it was parked, and pled for them to start slowly and not go faster than a few miles per hour, Sav would go out after dark and hide behind cars parked on the side of the street, and then wait for a car to come down the block and run behind it while crouching down until he was able to jump and grab onto the rear bumper. Then he would latch on and skeech for blocks and blocks, undetected by the driver. Typically he would find an old pair of my Mom's boots with the most warn out, slickest bottoms, as this would make for a better, faster ride.

He didn't care what he looked like, or who saw him. Or maybe he cared incredibly and just wanted to stand out by being more bizarre than the other kids. Sav never seemed to care what anyone thought of him. He was the 1970's version of X-Games before they even existed. He built ramps to jump with his ten speed bike, or grabbed other kid's bikes and would ghost ride them by riding them as fast as possible, then jumping off and letting the bike continue out of control until it careened into a wall or fence with incredible force.

My parents attempted to channel Sav's reckless abandon in a positive direction early on. They typecast him for wrestling at a young age since he was short, stocky and ornery. Though I later also took to the sport of wrestling, they initially encouraged me to play basketball given I was tall and lanky. After all, who ever heard of tall wrestlers or short basketball players? The problem with this method of assigning kids to sports was that Sav didn't much like wrestling in the long run, and I wasn't very good at basketball. There weren't many decent white basketball players in Dolton, and I certainly wasn't one of them.

Fred Marino, our wrestling coach, was a hard ass. He scared the shit out of me. It wasn't just that I weighed only a hundred pounds wet, but Coach had an intensity that was intimidating. He shifted his weight from side to side when he walked, and with fiery red hair he reminded me of the demonic Heat Miser character from "The Year Without a Santa Claus" cartoon.

"Walker, your intensity is for shit today. You better get after it or you'll be downstairs running with the sissy squad. I hear they need a white point guard with a mean reversal!" Marino yelled at me, then laughed as he walked by.

I don't remember why I chose wrestling as my sport of choice. Perhaps because Sav started wrestling when he was eight, and I saw how much attention it got him from Mom and Dad. I played Pop Warner football for six years before high school, but my weight made football a long shot. The T.R. football team was mostly black kids from Harvey, a nearby suburb described by our parents as a scary ghetto where white people got shot at just for driving through. So, absent football, basketball and baseball—Dad always said baseball players were big whiney babies anyway—I was left with the only sport where most white kids still made the team, people in school thought we were tough so they didn't mess with us, and the "wrestlerette" cheerleaders were pretty hot.

"Walker! Where's your brother? He's missed two practices again this week already," Coach Marino yelled as he entered the locker room.

"I don't know, Coach, I think out in his car getting his gear," I replied, half-correct since I knew he was in his car, but not getting his gear. I think this was my attempt to help Sav relieve himself of the pressure of playing a sport I knew he hated. He had already quit, now he just needed to make it official.

"That's it. I'm going to light a little fire under his ass," Coach Marino declared as he stomped off, running his fingers through the front of his red hair as he always did when he was fired up about something.

I ran to the window to see what happened next. Coach opened the door of Sav's beat-up car, revealing a plume of smoke and Sav sitting there drinking a beer and having a cigarette. A brief conversation ensued, then Coach closed the door and returned to the wrestling room.

"Your brother has decided wrestling is not for him anymore. What a fucking waste."

While Sav was once a promising wrestler as a kid, after middle school he stopped applying himself, despised practice, and didn't care. The beginning of the end was on preview night his sophomore year when Coach called the two of us out to execute a few moves in front of the visiting parents. I got the best of him that night, much to his and everyone's surprise, even though as a freshman I was new to the sport. I felt really bad afterward. I wanted him to be a superstar, I wanted my big brother to excel. He just didn't want it himself.

By the time he was a junior in high school, Sav was done with organized sports, taking instead to drinking beer and smoking cigarettes most weekends and many weekdays after school. He spent his senior year earning grades just good enough to get by, and after graduation he enrolled in the United States Army, which my folks decided "would be good for him." They were right; the army was good for him in terms of a steady paycheck and keeping him out of jail. But it only reinforced, if not accelerated, his use of drugs and alcohol.

After completing basic training at Ft. Bragg, Sav was home for Thanksgiving weekend. Mom had planned a nice turkey dinner for us, but come dinner time Sav was nowhere to be found. I grabbed my coat and the car keys. I had an idea where he might be. Behind Kmart was a huge field where they hadn't begun to build houses yet. Just trees, thick brush, and some trails that kids rode their motocross bikes on. At night it was pitch black, and we would sneak there to drink beer, light a campfire, and look at *Penthouse* magazines. This is where I knew to look for Sav whenever he disappeared.

As I entered the edge of the field and passed under the dense shrubbery, I stopped to see if I could hear anything or anyone nearby. It was incredibly quiet, and the November night air was still but freezing cold. The absence of wind made for perfect conditions for a fire. I exhaled crystallized breath into the air and continued toward the center of the prairie.

Then I heard what sounded like the crackling of fire in the distance, and I spotted a faint light about thirty yards ahead. I zig-zagged toward the orange ember, and as I got closer I could see what looked from behind to be a person kneeling down and praying. As I approached the silhouette, I recognized it was Sav kneeling near a roaring campfire shrouded among a thick tree line, unsteadily attempting to light the end of a stick in order to get it hot enough to light the cigarette hanging from his lips.

"What's up Sav? Mom and dad are wondering where you are," I said.

"Dude, can you get me another beer from the bucket? I'm trying to light my cigarette and I don't have any fucking matches."

Just then he raised a stick that was resting in the base of the fire, its end glowing red hot from the embers of the flames it was engulfed in. Without hesitation, Sav brought the makeshift torch toward his face in an attempt to light his cigarette. But the alcohol limited his dexterity and clouded his coordination, and along with the freezing elements removed any hope of successfully executing such an act. He missed the tip of the cigarette badly and instead pushed the red-hot poker against his cheek. My ears received the same sound as when my dad discarded his lit matches into the toilet when smoking in the bathroom.

"Holy shit, Sav. Are you crazy?" I yelled as I saw his singed skin turn a burnt black.

"What? Do you have any matches?" was his reply, seemingly unfazed by the burn to his face. I could tell he was drunker than usual, meaning he had at least a twelve-pack or more. Sav drank so often that at seventeen he could drink a six-pack no problem, and he could easily drink half a case before feeling a buzz.

"I've got matches in the car. Let's go have a few beers at home where it's warm. Mom and dad are going to be pissed."

David stumbled to his feet, chugged the rest of the beer he was holding, then tossed the empty can into the fire. "Don't worry, little brother. The juice is worth the squeeze."

I coaxed Sav to come home, and my parents just shook their heads in disbelief, reassured that after the weekend David would again be Uncle Sam's problem, not theirs. It's not as though they entirely gave up on David. They just seemed exhausted in terms of their effort to try to motivate him in a positive direction.

The following summer on a weekend camping outing at France Park, Indiana, where my friends and I went for one last bash before I left for college, Sav's love for beer and campfires again coincided. He had driven all night from his base at Bragg just to spend two days with the boys, and was already drunk when he pulled into our campsite. Everyone mobbed the Sav, and he popped the trunk of his Ford Fairmont, which held three cases of Red, White, and Blue. Everyone cheered, and we drank around the fire until near three in the morning. Eventually everyone crawled into a tent to crash, except Sav. The next morning, actually closer to noon by the time everyone came to, we awoke to find him still passed out on his side next to the campfire, his eyebrows and eyelids singed off from the nearby flames and half his face already sunburned. He woke up, reached for a cigarette and popped a fresh beer, and asked, "So what the fuck are we doing today?"

I wasn't old enough or mature enough to see that David was self-destructing. Like a jester dancing near a cliff, I was self-destructing in some ways too. Unsure about my future, unmotivated, driven by the base pleasures of alcohol and girls, and more invested in having fun than taking life seriously, I found David a mutual bedfellow during our teenage years. He protected me, and he made me laugh.

Sav hooked up with lots of girls in high school. He was especially well-endowed compared to most kids his age, which attracted many girls. Just before going into the service, he had been dating a girl named Lori who was two years younger than him. They saw each other on and off while he was doing his service time, and he saw her regularly whenever he was in town. But when he returned home for his second Christmas break since joining the Army, the first of two bombs were dropped on him.

"Dave, you're too wild for me. My parents want me to go to college and find a nice boy to be with. You're not what they have in mind," Lori told him while sitting in his car in our driveway on Christmas Eve.

Later that evening the doorbell rang as we were getting ready for church. Tracy, a girl he hung out with from time to time when he was back in town, stood on our front porch with a newborn in her arms.

"David, do you know this girl at the front door? She's asking for you," said Mom. "Please come in. It's freezing outside," my Mom said, ushering the girl and baby inside. My other brothers and I convened in the living room for the show.

"I know this is weird, but I heard David was back in town so I just wanted him to meet his daughter," Tracy said, as she turned to show us our new family member—baby Theresa.

My folks made the best of it, trying to say the right things versus freaking out. Instead of going to church that night, as was our Christmas Eve tradition, we stayed home and got to know Tracy and Theresa better. They left around ten o'clock, after which Sav said he needed to run out to get some air. When I went to bed a few hours later, he was still out.

I woke on Christmas morning feeling bad for Sav. First his girlfriend breaks up with him on Christmas Eve, then a few hours later he learns he has a daughter he never knew about. Sav and I were close, even though we were different in nearly every way. I wanted to do what I could to try to help him make sense of it all. I popped out of bed and saw that his bed was empty. In fact, it didn't look like he had slept there at all. When you spend day after day in the same little room as a brother or sister, they become part of you. You become intuitively connected beyond your mutual bloodline, and you share an emotional tie that permeates your hearts and minds. So if I was in trouble, he was there without me needing to define my situation or ask for help. When he was in trouble, I returned the favor.

Everyone else was still asleep, so I slipped out to try to find him. His car was still in the driveway, but he was gone. I drove around, checking all the usual spots, a few friends' houses and the Kmart field. He was nowhere to be found. I started to worry, and figured maybe my parents got a call in the night that would explain his whereabouts. As I pulled into our driveway Sav emerged from the house across the street where a divorcee named Suzi in her thirties lived. He had no jacket on, and he stumbled across the icy street and fell down as I closed the car door and approached him. He was drunker than I had ever seen him.

"Where the hell have you been all night?"

"Ize fugen miz dat bizh," was all he could articulate.

"What?" I said.

"I godda get Lori bag cause I cand live withow her and I fuckin love dat bitch," came his slightly better attempt to speak.

I placed his arm behind my neck to support his weight and carried him toward our front door. Sav giggled as we walked, and I could barely stand the combined smell of booze and cigarettes on his breath.

"Bulzeye," he said as he pushed on the door handle centered in the middle of our front door. I could tell he had been up all night, partying with Suzi and a few other burnouts from the block. My Dad was already in the kitchen, and just shook his head as he saw us enter.

"Late night, huh guys?"

"I just got up actually. Sav was across the street and needs some sleep."

"Jesus, David. On Christmas morning and after all our drama last night." Mom, fully exasperated, said mostly because she didn't know where to start. Dad was less sympathetic.

"Get yourself some coffee, David, or I'm throwing you out in the snow." I could tell Dad was tempted to grin at the sight of the Sav. But I think he too was reeling from last night's early Christmas gift—the unexpected arrival of his unanticipated first granddaughter.

Mom put coffee on and said, "David, I don't know why you do this to yourself. All over some girl. We'll work out the other situation. I mean, do we even know if that kid is actually yours?"

"Bud ah love that beetch, mom."

"Don't use that language, especially on Christmas. Anyway, which bitch? Lori, Tracy or Suzi? Really, you're enough to put me over the edge! Now, let's please have some meat pie and open our presents. We're heading to your cousins at noon," Mom directed. She was more rattled than usual. Her spiced French meat pie on holidays was a family tradition. But I think it was pretty clear that no holiday tradition was going to normalize things this year.

The rest of the morning was a combination of my Dad's hollow threats to throw David out of the house, Mom instructing him to go sleep it off, and Sav attempting to conquer the challenging task of opening Christmas presents while blind drunk and crying about his high school sweetheart leaving him and being informed he is the father of a girl whose mother he had little use for.

We departed for my cousins without Sav, who was finally asleep by the time we left the house. When we got home I ran downstairs to check on him. There was the Sav, out cold, fully naked and uncovered flat on his bed, legs dangling over the side, with several empty beer cans strewn about the bed. In one hand was a peanut butter and jelly sandwich, and in the other a photo of Lori.

THE HOT DOG MAN

Chief Walker made regular visits to the home of Dolton Mayor Donald J. Hart after Don became sick. But he never called him Don or Donny out of respect. Always "Mr. Mayor." The chief did his best to update the Mayor about what was happening in Dolton, about police matters and crime, resident issues and complaints, and about the trustee's meetings. Then he dutifully delivered the Mayor's notes, instructions and ideas on cassette tape back to the Village Hall. But each visit painted a grimmer picture of the once physically active and handsome man everyone in Dolton knew and loved. After only a few months with such a terrible disease, Don was unable to hold utensils, after six months he was unable to drive, and within ten months he was confined to a wheelchair in his home. He soon lost the ability to control his limbs at all. In the last months he couldn't speak or breathe on his own. On January 28, 1998, at sixty-three years of age, the man so many people knew as the Hot Dog Man was dead.

———————————

As Donny and Al entered the break room unzipping their coats to thaw out, a commotion ensued, and several foremen ran by them toward the meat processing room of the plant (also known as "the grind"). They overheard one say, "Jesus. Is the ambulance on the way? I can't believe Pete could lose his hand." They assumed this meant something happened to their friend, Pete Keys. They ran out of the break room and toward the processing room to check it out. A cluster of fellow workers were surrounding Pete, lying unconscious in a pool of blood. Pete and Al could never figure if it was called the grind because of the razor sharp grinder blades that mushed the meat into a disgusting pink substance, or because of the harsh conditions requiring lifting heavy meat parts onto the constantly moving conveyor belt. Pete's arm was covered in a fellow worker's shirt and jacket, but was already bleeding through.

99

"What is taking the paramedics so damn long? Come on man, we're gonna lose him!" one of the foremen shouted.

Just then several paramedics pushed through the crowd and began working on Pete. Donny looked over at the combine, where the meat was ground and would later be encased in hot dog sheaths. On the floor near the spinner blade was a blood-soaked hand. Pete's hand, no longer attached to his body.[2]

"Let's go, man. There's nothing we can do here," Al broke Donny's trance, pulling him out of the room and away from the image of the severed hand on the floor.

"Poor Pete. Someone needs to call his wife. She's pregnant and they just got an eviction notice because they aren't making their rent," Donny said as Al escorted him back toward the break room.

"Hygrade will take care of it. We'll call her tonight to check in, or have the girls stop by to see her. Don't worry. Come on, we need to get back to the dock," Al said, putting his knit cap back on and pulling it down over his ears, then stretching his work gloves back over his calloused hands.

"We *really* need to find another job, Al. That could have been one of us. Working an eight-hour shift then pulling overtime in the grind. I've found myself daydreaming as I've pushed the meat into the spinner. I mean, how the hell is Pete going to be able to continue work with only one god damn hand?"

When Donny got home that night, he was still shaken by the incident. All he could think about was spending the next thirty years at Hygrade. Would he look old and tired at forty-five like some of the guys who had been at the plant for too many years? Hunched over, out of shape, bones and muscles deteriorating prematurely due to physical labor and working in the cold? It pushed his mind to the brink of hopelessness, but the desperation also forced him to think about a better plan. Even a ridiculous idea was worth a shot. The next day at work was no better than the day of Pete's accident.

"Man Donny, I can't believe they've cut our overtime. How's a guy supposed to make ends meet with straight time?" Al asked, as he lifted another forty-pound box of sausage off the conveyer belt and onto a pallet. It was 6am and the temperature outside on the

---

[2] This aspect of the story is embellished. No injury of this nature occurred at Hygrade associated with the characters in this story.

dock was twenty-two degrees with a wind chill that made it feel like minus ten. Don couldn't make out most of what Al said, since the roar of the engine from the forklift was penetrating his ears. He turned it off, dismounted from the frozen plastic seat, and walked toward Al to help load the boxes onto the lift. He clapped his hands sharply a few times to keep the blood flowing, imitating a quarterback leaving a huddle.

"Say what?"

"I said, how are we going to get by without logging any overtime this month? That's three hundred bucks, and Christmas is just around the corner. I'm telling you, Hygrade is screwing us like squealing pigs!"

Don replied, "I'll talk to Stan. He's always taken care of us before. We've got decent seniority now, so I'm sure if orders increase this month we'll get some more hours. Besides, they can always use extra hands in the grind." Don stopped himself as the words left his mouth, feeling bad that he might have made a joke at Pete's expense. Al noticed Don's pause and tried to bail him out.

"Don't worry about it. I know what you mean. We'll help Pete and his family however we need to. But we just need to make ends meet."

Money was tight. It was 1969 and Don Hart and Al Premarty were dock workers at Hygrade Meat Factory on 23rd and Halsted in Chicago. After twelve years of 5:30am-2:30pm shifts, Don and Al were mentally and physically exhausted. Both in their early thirties, their day started with Al rising at 3:30 to catch a quick shower and pick up Donny at his house in Dolton around four, then a quick stop at Chris' Coffee Shop near the highway for coffee, then a forty-five minute ride into the city. The work at Hygrade was physically demanding, tedious, and stressful: Unloading heavy, frozen animal parts from freezer trucks and transferring them into the plant. Packing sausage and hot dogs for delivery, transferring the meat into boxes for binding, and then lifting each forty-pound box onto a pallet to be transferred on forklifts into trucks to be distributed throughout the Chicago and northwest Indiana area and beyond. An average of one incoming and three outgoing trucks an hour, at least thirty trucks a day. When orders were up, Donny and Al pulled overtime, at time and a half beyond their straight wage. But lately very little overtime was available.

But overtime work sometimes meant working on the other side of the factory, working in the slaughterhouse, known by the men as "the grind." The place where Pete likely spent his last shift at Hygrade. The animals were killed at various Illinois and Indiana hog and cattle farms; then their frozen carcasses were delivered in freezer trucks—rock solid sides of beef the shape of half-cows and full pigs weighing as much as a thousand pounds. Conveyor belts helped deliver the frozen meat from the trucks to the loading docks, but then the men carried them onto skids and wheeled them by hand to the carving rooms where the meat was sawed up and distributed for various products. Polish sausage, Italian sausage, hot dogs, and bratwurst, in addition to traditional hamburgers.

Donny and his wife Bert were raising four kids. He always wanted a big family, though he never understood just how expensive it was to feed a family of six. Donny put in three years in the Army after high school, while Al initially worked tear-offs for a roofing company in Hammond. But a near-death accident on a cold January morning where a toe-hold gave loose was enough to motivate him to find other work. Al was in good shape, perhaps a bit overweight, with dark hair and a full dark beard, and still walking with a slight limp from the accident. Donny was still in great physical shape. A muscular build, long blonde hair and a goatee, with a tattoo on his forearm that read "Bambino."

Bert was his best friend from childhood, and provided him the best support a stay-at-home wife could. She could have had a career, but elected instead to raise the kids and take care of the house on Dorchester Street. The schools were good and the neighborhood was safe, but in recent years she worried about Donny's stress level and how he seemed more exhausted from the work at the factory. He rarely complained, but she could tell it was getting tougher on him.

"Hey sweetie. How was your day? I bought your Schlitz this morning, and dinner will be ready soon," Bert said as Donny walked through the front door and kicked off his boots. He threw his gloves, hat, and jacket onto the coat hook near the front door, as six-year-old Donny Junior ran from the kitchen into his arms.

"Daddy! Did you make the meat today?" Donny Junior asked. Meanwhile Bert held one-year-old Jennifer on her hip while she stirred the mashed potatoes the best she could with one hand.

"Donny, don't fuss. Leave your dad to relax a bit," Bert said to Junior as she plopped Jennie into her high chair to free both arms to finish dinner. Theirs was a modest two-bedroom split level, a house Donny bought after being released from the service in 1956 a year before they married. Bert's dad lent him the money for the down payment, and the $15,000 price tag and monthly mortgage worried Donny even though his connections to an army buddy landed him the job at Hygrade right out of the service. It seemed like a sweet gig at first. A regular salary, health insurance and a pension. Plus his best friend Al Premarty had already been working there a year, so they could drive to and from work together.

"I'll tell you, babe, this work isn't getting any easier. No matter how many layers of clothes I wear, I freeze my ass off on that dock," Donny said, taking a seat at the table and reaching for the newspaper. "There's got to be work somewhere else that pays just as well."

"Daddy, what does freeze your ass off mean?" Donny Junior asked, awkwardly climbing up onto the seat next to his weary father.

Donny looked up from the newspaper, trying to hold back his laughter, and replied, "It means you're really, really cold. Now go wash your hands before dinner."

It was a Tuesday evening, mid-December, and the thought of three more cold days at work before the weekend had Donny on edge. Bert sensed as much, and put the last pot of food on the table before giving Donny a hug from behind as he reached for a spoonful of potatoes.

"You'll figure something out. You always do," Bert whispered, then kissed Donny's neck.

That night the sex between Donny and Bert was good. They held hands the whole time just as they did as teenagers when they snuck off around every corner just to be together. She laid her head on Donny's firm chest as he reached over for a cigarette.

"Al is worried there won't be overtime this month. And after Pete's accident I'm not sure I want to push for extra hours in the grind."

"I'm not helpless you know, I can get a job. Mom can come keep an eye on the kids most days," Bert said smiling, though she knew what Donny's reply would be.

"No way. You have enough stuff going on with the kids. I will make it work as I always do. I can always pull some work on weekends helping old man Fabrie with construction, or Butch Sikora with S&K Builders. I'm a damn good carpenter you know."

"Let's just see how it goes, babe. I like spending time with you and the kids on weekends. More work means less time with us." Donny finished his cigarette as Bert hugged his stomach and settled in. She was confident she would be able to help him manage the pressures of his job as she always could.

As Donny reached over to turn off the light, he recognized that for the first time in his life he was feeling a bit suffocated. A bit trapped. Kids, work pressure, bills…it was all becoming a bit much to manage.

The next morning was colder than usual. Donny woke to WGN weather on his alarm clock, same as every day. It helped him know whether he would need thermal underwear, an extra hooded sweatshirt, and an extra pair of socks. The only hope to keep the biting Chicago cold from freezing his skin was multiple layers. The men who worked on the Hygrade docks had no other protection. In the summers, which were hot and humid, it also meant knowing how to stay cool. The summers were also difficult because of the smell. The hot temperatures had a way of making the Hygrade plant reek of butchered meat that enveloped the factory, the men, and the clothes they wore. Some days Donny and Al would throw their pants and shirts in the trunk before driving home, just to avoid dragging the stench along with them.

Today's forecast called for a high of fifteen degrees and a chance of sleet or freezing rain. Donny knew this meant Al would be there early to pick him up. Bad weather meant back-ups on the Dan Ryan Expressway, and back-ups meant the chance of being late. Hygrade had no tolerance for tardiness. More than two tardies in any fiscal quarter meant docked pay, and the next tardy meant termination. Neither Donny or Al could afford such predicaments, so they left as early as necessary according to the daily forecast.

Al took a long drag from his cigarette as Donny hopped in Al's beat up Dodge Dart. They alternated driving from week to week, and as crappy as Al's car was it had a working heater, which was all that mattered.

"Morning big guy. Ready for another glorious day?" Donny said as he threw his lunch pail in the back and hopped into the front seat.

"I was thinking. Friday is payday, so we really need to go out and have a few beers. We can take the girls to a show on Saturday, but on Friday we need to go check out that new waitress at Romar's," Al said as he sped from the curb in front of Don's house.

"Whatever. I just need to get through this week without killing someone. I mean, first our overtime is cut and now the forecast is for freezing rain and snow the rest of the week. What a shitty deal," Donny said, lighting his cigarette and cranking down his window just enough to let the smoke escape. He reached to fiddle with the radio dial as he always did, turning the tuner knob until he found his favorite rock station- WLUP.

"Sweet! Jethro Tull," Donny exhaled smoke as he moved his head and shoulders to the beat of Bungle in the Jungle.

The traffic was slow as expected, but they made it to work a few minutes before 5:30. By seven, they had already finished loading five trucks and were heading inside for a ten-minute break. Ten minutes to grab a hot cup of coffee and try to thaw out their cold bodies from several hours of exposure. Hardly enough time to take a piss, they always joked. The mood was somber that day, everyone talking of Pete's accident. Donny arrived home that night more desperate than usual, feeling as though another day at Hygrade could put him over the edge.

"Bert, have you still been going to that little farm stand in the lot at the corner of Cottage Grove and 142nd?"

"About once a week, mostly because their fruits and vegetables are cheaper than Sterks. Why?"

"Didn't you say you talk to the guy who owns it sometimes? What's his name again, Anthony?"

"Anthony Gilmartin. Yeah, we talk sometimes. He's a nice old man. Why? What's on your mind?" Bert could see that Donny's wheels were turning.

"Stop by there tomorrow. Ask Anthony if he can give me a few minutes of his time Saturday morning. I have an idea I want to pitch to him."

By Saturday, the image of Pete's accident was still haunting Donny. He hadn't discussed his idea with Al since he'd mentioned it in passing months ago, but now he was prepared to run it by Anthony and see what he thought. It was a bit warmer Saturday morning, at least by Chicago standards—around 38 degrees—so Donny took his time picking out a few items from Anthony's farm stand, a single wooden structure on a large vacant lot that sat at a busy intersection in Dolton. There were fewer options in the winter, but still some nice produce, jellies, and locally baked Wonder bread. There weren't many customers in the winter, but in the spring and summer they did steady business. Donny was smart to load a few extra things into his basket in order to make a nice purchase of Anthony's goods before talking business with him.

"Mr. Gilmartin, my name is Don Hart. We met last summer when I was here purchasing watermelons for a family picnic. My wife Bert comes here all the time. Can I talk to you about something?" Donny asked as he paid for his produce.

Anthony's parents had emigrated from Italy to Chicago years ago, and his father ran a printing press for the *Chicago Sun Times*. He was around sixty, a portly fellow with a great disposition, always smiling and speaking in broken English. He paid a modest rent to the Piscateers fishing club to sell produce and other food items on the vacant gravel lot just outside the fence to the lake on property own by Piscateers. He did well because his customers liked him.

"Si. Bert ah already tell me you want to talk. Ay stay up late ah last night, having some beers, watching the Blackhawks. I needah another cup of coffee. Wantah some?" Anthony asked as he wiped his hands on his apron and waved for one of his workers to cover the register.

"Sure. Thanks," Donny said as he followed Anthony to the back of the store, where a coffee pot and styrofoam cups sat on a stack of old wooden lettuce boxes. Coffee was free for customers, a little perk Anthony provided to help get people in the door.

Donny took a deep breath before beginning. He only had one chance to get it right, and he was no salesman. He tried to hide his emotion as he began. This wasn't just a brainchild, it was his future.

"Here's the thing. This spring when the weather breaks, I'd like to set up a little stand on your lot to sell hot dogs. I think I can get a good deal on them in large supply from the place I work, and I think your customers might buy them as they're purchasing your stuff. I've got to try something to make more money for my family, and possibly find something else to do other than work downtown every day. I work outside mostly, and the work is difficult."

"I see. My father work for the *Sun Times* outside ah for years. He, ah, provided for our family after he come over from Italia. He give me ah the money to start this business twenty years now," Anthony said, his broken English now more decipherable to Donny after conversing for a few minutes.

Anthony was intrigued by the idea. He was no genius, but he liked the idea of having a second business on the lot to draw more customers. They weren't selling similar items, so he didn't figure it would hurt his business any. But why take the chance, he wondered. His business was doing fine.

"Interesting. I guessah my only worry I have is ifah people come to spend their money on my stuff, but justah come to buy your stuff. Let me think it over. Maybe, ah, we can try out for a few months. See what happens. I needah to check with the lake. You know, the Piscateers. They ownah the lot. I just pay the rent. You know, they'll want rent money from you too."

Donny could see that Anthony liked the idea, and he held direct eye contact with him as he spoke. His broken English made him hard to follow, but Donny got the sense that Anthony might help him make it happen. He seemed like a straight-shooter, and he trusted him from the start.

"I call you after I speak to lake men. You say hi for your wife for me, and I call soon."

Even the prospect of this new venture had Donny upbeat by the time he got home. They lived only half a mile from Anthony's. He placed the groceries on the table and yelled for Bert.

"Bert! Hey, there you are. I think Anthony liked the idea. Man, how sweet would it be for us to make some extra cash and maybe for me to eventually get out of that damn factory."

"That's great. Let me know how I can help," Bert said as she gave Donny a hug and kept moving with Jennie in her arms and four-year-old Chris trailing close behind. Kim, twelve, and Donny Jr. entered the room together curious about the discussion.

"What are you guys talking about?" Kim asked. "Is daddy getting a new job?"

"What are you going to do daddy?" Donny Jr. asked.

"Nothing for you guys to worry about. Daddy doesn't need a new job. Everything is fine. Help take Chris in and wash her hands, Kimmy. Donny, you too. Get ready for dinner," Bert instructed.

With the prospect of the spring experiment looming, the late winter days at the factory seemed longer than ever. Each day dragged by, with Al and Donny struggling to maintain their enthusiasm. Al wanted out of the factory as much as Don, and he embraced the idea of the hot dog stand at least as a means of making some extra cash. Donny never thought twice about asking Al to help with the venture. They had been friends since high school, and they did everything together. Don also figured having two families putting up the initial investment was safer than going it alone.

The additional overtime hours they'd hoped for hadn't come, so money was tight for both families. But a few nights a week Al would come over with Virginia, his wife, and the four of them would continue to plan for how they would start the hot dog stand. Opening weekend was to be Saturday, April first. The plan was to try weekends first. One night as they discussed how much food they would need for opening weekend, the phone rang. Donny answered it and the others in the room could tell the news was bad.

"Yes. Hi Anthony. How are you?" Donny started.

"What! One-fifty per month? Why so high?" Donny tried to remain calm, but struggled to keep his composure.

"Insurance? I'm going to be selling boiled hot dogs and potato chips and some cans of pop. Why do I need insurance?"

"I see. Yes, we will be using propane to heat the burners," Donny became calmer as Anthony explained the terms provided by Piscateers. Virginia, Al, and Bert sat quietly listening to the conversation, piecing together what was happening. Then Donny hung up.

"It's going to cost us two hundred per month to use the lot. One-fifty for rent and fifty for insurance. I don't see how we can do it," Donny said, dejected, returning to the kitchen table where the others were sitting.

Bert was the only one among them with any education beyond high school, having received her Associates Degree from Thornton Community College while Donny was in the service. She had a business savvy about her that she didn't get to practice much as a stay-at-home mom. She addressed the others calmly and confidently.

"Let's just do the math and see how it looks," she said while reaching for a piece of paper and pencil.

"Hygrade is selling us the hot dogs at cost plus ten percent, which is twenty-five dollars per box. There are four hundred hot dogs in each box. We're getting potato chips from Frito-Lay direct, at ten cents per bag and planned for eighty bags for opening weekend, so that's eight dollars. The buns are forty cents per bag with eight buns per bag, so we'll need fifty bags for each case of hot dogs. That's another twenty bucks."

The others sat in amazement as she threw out the numbers and did the math in her head, without the use of a calculator or even adding or subtracting anything on the page. She tapped the back of the pencil against her temple as she added the numbers out loud for the others.

"Then we were going to purchase five cases of Canfield's soda, which gives us a hundred and twenty cans of pop for opening weekend, at a cost of two dollars per case. We figure maybe we'll spend another twenty dollars on condiments—mustard, relish, onions, tomatoes, and cucumbers—which by the way Anthony is selling us at a great price. So our total cost for opening weekend is around eighty-five dollars, give or take. If we add the fifty dollars per weekend that Piscateers is requiring for rent and insurance, our cost for the weekend is around a hundred and ten."

"No way. We'll lose our shirts!" Al chimed in, standing up and making his way to the fridge to open another beer. "How many of those damn wieners will we need to sell to even break even?"

"Wait man, just hear her out," Donny said. "So how much do we plan to charge for what we're selling?"

Bert continued, "I think the best bet is to sell all three items together. A hot dog, small bag of chips and a soda for a dollar fifty, or just a hot dog alone for a dollar. If we purchase enough supply for opening weekend to sell a few hundred meals, we'll cover our costs *and* turn a profit."

Donny reached for one of Al's cigarettes and lit it. He seemed to be smoking more lately, not just as he used to which was only if he was having a few beers or when he was really on edge. He exhaled toward the light hanging over the kitchen table, leaning back in his chair.

"That's a lot of work for only a little money," Donny said.

"Right, but that's one weekend. If sales are good, that means four times that amount per month. We could make several hundred dollars per month per family. That's not bad," Bert dropped the pencil and looked up at the others.

"What do you guys think?" Donny directed his question toward Al and Virginia.

Al answered for both of them without hesitation: "We're in."

After the long wait, April first finally arrived. Both families showed up at the lot early that morning to set up. They pitched a small tent, under which they placed a double Coleman grill on a small table. A few smaller tables were set up to hold the rest of the food and a cash box. They brought several coolers of ice for the pop, and by ten they were ready to go. A small sign hanging from the tent gave the only indication of what they were selling: "Fresh Hot Dogs."

But the day was overcast, and as the farm stand customers pulled into the lot, most just looked over toward the tent and proceeded into Anthony's. Anthony came out around eleven and greeted the group as a light rain started to fall.

"Goodah mornin. I want to be your firstah customah. Everything on mine, per favore," he said, giving Bert two dollars. She creased one of the dollars and placed it in the cash box, smiling back at Anthony as Donny pulled a hot dog from the steaming water and placed it in a fresh bun.

"May this dollar have plenty of company from here forward," Bert declared as she placed it in the box.

"Everything on it?" Donny asked.

"Si. Run it through the garden," Anthony replied, drawing laughter from the kids trying earnestly to help their parents but mostly just getting in the way. "Ah, Grazie. Is likeah a work of art. Picasso would be proud."

He was right. It was no regular hot dog. The yellow mustard, bright green relish, diced white onion, wedges of fresh red tomato, and striped green cucumber gave it incredible color. It truly was a work of art, and Anthony devoured it in several bites under the tent, then ordered several more for his staff before returning back to the farm stand at the back of the lot.

As the afternoon went on, a few of Anthony's customer wandered out to buy lunch, mostly at Anthony's urging. At five o'clock, as Anthony flipped the sign in his window from "Open" to "Closed," Bert could see the disappointment in Donny's eyes.

"How much?" Donny asked Al as he counted the cash in the box.

"Thirty-six dollars."

Bert sensed everyone's despair, but remained calm. She offered up the best explanation she could muster. "It's our first day, guys. And the weather hurt us. Every day forward will get better."

They packed everything up and loaded the cars. They would be back on the lot tomorrow, Sunday, after church. Breaking even on opening weekend was a long shot.

The following day brought brilliant sunshine, and the kids made some colorful signs and glued them to little wooden rulers to put on the side of the road. Kim's signs read, "Stop for a yummy lunch!" and "Delicious hot dogs." Donny Jr., who watched the Bozo's Circus Show on television every day, wrote, "Bozo the clown eats here!"

On the second day business was better. People stopping for fresh produce were curious about what was happening under the little tent on the corner. The smell of boiling hot dogs wafted through the parking lot, and seeing people eating and drinking a cold can of pop enticed others to buy. By five o'clock Sunday they knew they had done better than opening day.

"Eighty-four dollars and fifty cents. That makes one hundred and twenty for the weekend. This means we didn't break even. We're about a hundred short from even breaking even!" Al panicked, looking at Bert as he tossed the cash back into the cash box.

She implored him to be reasonable. "C'mon Al. How many businesses are immediately successful? We're going to need to be patient, and—"

"Be patient! We're already borrowing money from our family this month just to pay for the food and rent. If we don't turn a profit in four weeks, I'm screwed."

"I know. Let's feed the kids and eat before we pack up. Then we'll head back to the house and talk about how to improve things for next weekend." Bert attempted to calm Al down. She had emerged as the figurehead of the fledging business, and felt obligated to jump-start things. As she walked along the road to clean up, Donny Junior's sign caught her eye: "Bozo the clown eats here."

The talk about changes for next weekend brought the group some optimism. Bert pitched the idea of a name that would resonate with nearly everyone. The next day Virginia drove to the *Dolton Tattler* and placed an ad to run on Tuesday and Thursday, announcing the opening of "Bozo's Hot Dog Stand." A friend of Al's delivered two picnic benches, each able to seat ten people, along with some large umbrellas to provide shade. Stan at Hygrade permitted Donny to buy two empty fifty-five gallon metal barrels to use as trash cans. The kids painted them after school- orange and yellow stripes. Bert worked all week on a large cardboard sign nailed to two large wooden posts which Donny and Al staked into the ground at the corner of the lot. The kids also painted the sign in bright orange and yellow colors: "Bozo's Hot Dogs."

The following weekend came, and still things were slow at first. Saturday's cash total was just above last Saturday's, and Sunday's was about the same. Bert was feeling desperate, and the disappointment on Donny's face had her worried. As she helped pack up for the day she looked across the street on the other side of Cottage Grove at the enormous factory with its parking lot full of cars for the hundreds of workers of Kaiser Aluminum. She had an idea, but decided not to share it with the others.

"Sweetie, I have to stop at the store on the way home. Have Al and Virginia drop you off and I'll be home shortly," Bert said as she hovered around the tent waiting for the others to leave. She walked across the street and into Kaiser's main office.

The following Saturday a few customers trickled in around noon. Then a group of workers with Kaiser uniforms walked up, followed by a few more, followed by yet more. Bert looked up to see a long line of factory workers from Kaiser waiting for lunch.

"Bert. What's this coupon they have for a hot dog, chips and a soda for a dollar?" Donny asked.

"It's the start of our little company," Bert replied.

Al looked toward Bert and shot her a big smile as he placed another hot dog into a bun and passed it to Virginia for its toppings. Between serving two customers he grabbed Bert by the arm and hugged her, and whispered, "You're a genius. You really saved us."

Donny walked over and hugged Bert and Al, and said, "Goodbye to the docks. But we need to call Stan and see if he can let us pick up a few more cases of dogs!"

The last customer was served at five, the agreed upon closing time in their lease, and Donny and Al each began counting the cash. The cash box was filled to the top with single dollar bills, but also plenty of fives, tens, and even a few twenties.

"One eighty," Donny reported to the group, looking toward Al anxiously to wait on his amount.

"Sixteen, seventeen, eighteen. Two eighteen!" Al shouted.

Both families erupted in cheer. Al and Donny slapped hands and Bert and Virginia hugged.

"Nearly four hundred in one day! I would have never dreamed we would have such success already," Donny said as he approached Bert and they kissed.

From that day forward word spread that a few Dolton residents were trying to get a new business started. Friends from church, families that went to the same schools as the kids, and a number of police and firefighters came out to support the business. Each weekend the income was higher than the previous.

Donny developed a system where the kids pulled fresh produce from one cooler, rinsed and chopped it on a table at the back of the tent, then rotated it onto the main serving table for Al and Donny to use. Donny kept careful watch on the hot dogs as they simmered, making sure to keep enough cooked and ready to serve, without running low. Kim and Donny Junior transferred ice into the coolers of soda, and made sure there were plenty of napkins. Al's two sons helped empty the trash barrels as they became full. The addition of the picnic tables was a big hit, and many customers purchased a second hot dog after tasting the first. There was no one else in town selling hot dogs like this. The combined ingredients made for a uniquely delicious taste.

Each weekend was progressively busier, and soon residents from the surrounding communities were coming into Dolton for

Bozo's Hot Dogs. Anthony's business also improved, and eventually he had trouble keeping enough produce in stock to meet demand. After the first month they easily cleared their overhead, and each family banked nearly six hundred dollars. May and June were even better. Their lease was good through Labor Day, and even the hot summer days of July and August never slowed their flow of new and returning customers. By the end of summer, they began making plans for the following year, and discussed erecting a small wooden shack on the lot and keeping it open every day, just like Anthony's Produce.

So they entered into an agreement to erect a wooden structure on the corner of the lot, twelve feet by fifteen, with a large open window at the front over a counter top four feet from the ground. The opening was designed so a large piece of plywood on hinges could be flipped up and propped open, exposing a long Formica tabletop inside where the food would be prepared. A steam table was placed in the back corner, ignited by propane and large enough to hold up to 50 hot dogs at a time, with a side compartment for steaming the buns. Donny's friend designed a metal rack that held eight hot dogs at a time, so they could be loaded with condiments without tipping over, and he also created a chip rack where small bags of potato chips could be clipped and displayed. This way the customers could choose from a variety of types of chips and pull off whichever bag they wanted.

Outside the shack was a large stainless steel water trough, like those you might see outside a horse barn. This would be filled with blocks of ice and could hold as many as ten cases of soda at a time. The cash box was replaced with a small cash register and 10-key adding machine, where the bills could be kept in order for making quick change.

The plan was to have the new structure ready for the April first opening, and Donny and Al put in for their annual two-week vacation to experiment with keeping Bozo's open every day. If after two weeks it appeared they could make enough money to equal their salaries at the plant, they would quit Hygrade and go into the hot dog business full time. They calculated the risk and knew they would be rolling the dice to make it work. But the thought of leaving the morning commute, freezing on the dock and hard labor at

Hygrade elevated their optimism. Donny kept reminding himself over and over, *it will all work out. It just has to.*

While Al and Donny began construction of the structure, including adding four more picnic tables and designing a bigger sign, Bert and Virginia took care of marketing and advertising. They placed ads in newspapers in Dolton, Calumet City, and South Holland, and included different coupons that could be cut out and presented by the customers for rebates. Buy one hot dog, get the second for twenty five cents. Buy two meals, and get a free soda. Bert even developed a punch card system, where after a customer purchased nine hot dogs, the tenth was free. She had a knack for business, and each of the four owners pulled their weight. Virginia convinced the editor of the South Holland *Shopper* newspaper to run a feature story on the grand opening.

April first finally arrived, and the parking lot was full of cars and eager customers an hour before ten, the new opening time. Some were coming back to taste again the delicious food they had last summer. Others were coming for the first time, having heard about the new hot dog stand outside Anthony's Produce. After the first weekend, the cash receipts were in excess of eight hundred dollars. The weekdays were just as busy, and Donny's friends working for the Village of Dolton Municipal Department convinced them to open earlier in the morning to serve hot coffee and doughnuts as well as the food items for people coming off the night shift. The large gravel parking lot was perfectly suited to accommodate large service vehicles and construction trucks. Road workers, garbage men, firefighters and cops all made their morning stop at Bozo's, and many came back for lunch later in the day.

By Wednesday evening Al and Donny made up their mind: they were going into the hot dog business full time. No more freezing dock in the Chicago winters, no more sitting in traffic on the Dan Ryan, no more sweating in the middle of summer, no more dealing with the stench of the factory and dangerous work in the grind.

"You call first, and I'll call next. Hell, who cares. We might as well call together. Stan is going to flip!" Al said as they climbed into his car after closing up.

"At least we're going to give them plenty of business buying their stuff," Donny said smiling. "It's a win-win situation."

"Let's hit Castaways to celebrate. I haven't used the new bowling ball Bert got me for my birthday. And we can have a few beers and relax a bit. No more 4am alarm clock from now on!" Al yelled out his window as they drove away from the stand, the colorful Bozo's sign reflecting the setting evening sun in his rearview mirror.

Donny closed Al's car door and flicked his cigarette onto the street outside his house. As Al pulled away, Donny whistled the chorus from Sweet Caroline as he stumbled toward his front door. It was two in the morning, and he zig-zagged across his front lawn and fumbled for his keys on his porch. The reflection in the window of the front door showed bright red lipstick on his neck. He quickly reached for his handkerchief and wiped it away. Bert was surely fast asleep by now anyway. He looked forward to sleeping in and then playing with the kids in the morning.

Business improved month after month, and it quickly became clear they would need more space. Hygrade was now delivering two cases of hotdogs per day, and the refrigerator in the stand they built was barely large enough to contain all the meat and produce. Daily delivery of ice was expensive and inefficient, and they were running electricity from Anthony's building and paying him an additional monthly amount. The stand had limited running water, so they needed to bring home the dishes and utensils every night to clean them at home. The Code Enforcement Officer had already warned them that they had one year to meet Code requirements, including sanitation rules, or they would need to close.

"I think we need to buy Anthony out," Bert said to Donny one night at dinner.

"What? Can we afford to?" Donny replied, though he knew his wife had already thought things through.

"We can't afford not to. We need to offer him more than he makes right now, and offer to pay it to him over time. Anthony's health isn't great, and running that produce store is a lot of work. I think if we dangle the right carrot in his direction, he'll bite," Bert said confidently. "Then we need to design a restaurant that meets

Code requirements, has a small business office on site, a walk-in refrigerator, and public restrooms for customers. We can offer a broader range of meals and extend our hours a bit. Frankly, we need to also get Piscateers to the table and buy the lot versus pay them rent."

"And you've done the math on all this? Have you consulted the Premartys? You know Al is really tight with his end of the money. I'm not sure he's ready for all this," Donny replied.

"When you remind him that Code Enforcement has us on a short leash and if we don't comply he will be back at Hygrade freezing his ass off on that dock, he'll do whatever we tell him to."

Bert's business confidence made Donny feel secure. He had a blue collar work ethic, but not a natural brain for business. Bert had both. He knew in his heart he wasn't in love with his wife as he once was. They weren't intimate like they used to be. But she was a great mother and business partner, and he had no desire to leave his family. His occasional extramarital flings sometimes made him feel guilty, but he reminded himself he was a good provider for his family, and loved them as much as any father did. So what if he had a few girlfriends on the side, he thought. He always came home at night and always took care of Bert and the kids.

So by the end of the second spring, plans were in place for building the restaurant. They qualified for a small business loan, and even the people at the bank were already regular customers at Bozo's, and Donny and Al had friends in the construction business to help keep the cost of building the restaurant down. Donny's buddy Butch Sikora ran point on the design and construction, and Anthony accepted Bert's offer to buy him off the lot. The landlords didn't budge on the request to sell the lot, knowing that they could enjoy years of rent from the restaurant, given its popularity and prospects for a bright future.

The new restaurant was to be set back on the lot far enough that they were able to keep the existing store open while building the new one. It was October, and construction was nearly complete when the strange envelope with a return address that read "WGN Television" came in the Harts' mailbox. Bert opened it and immediately knew it was bad news. The top of the letter included the following phrase in capitals and bold: CEASE AND DESIST IMMEDIATELY. The body of the letter read-

"WGN Broadcasting has become aware that you are illegally using a trademarked name to operate a business in Dolton, IL. The term 'Bozo' is a registered and protected name for the clown who performs on The Bozo Show. You are hereby ordered to cease and desist any and all use of this term associated with your business. Failure to do so will result in pending civil legal action, including monetary damages, between WGN and your business."

Bert thought through the best way to tell Donny, Al and Virginia. She invited the Premartys to dinner that night and informed them of the letter.

"Great. Now we need to change the name and we've just got started," Al said, pushing his chair away from the dinner table.

"People already know who we are, and what we offer. The name isn't as important anymore," Bert said as she removed the dirty dishes from the table and placed them in the sink.

"Screw that clown! The signs are already done. Let's just put a smiley face in the last o in the name and call it Boz. We can use the same colors as before, and as long as we keep making great food people won't care what we're called," Donny said, rising from his seat to help clear the table.

Bert went the following day to consult with a family friend who was an attorney. His office was just three blocks from Piscateers, on Chicago Avenue in downtown Dolton. James Miner Legal Services was the only place in Dolton for legal advice, though they mostly handled divorces, wills, and contracts. James was a handsome man, did a stint as an actor in L.A. before completing law school at the University of Chicago. By Dolton standards, he was one of the most educated and respected men in town. He also had a great sense of humor.

"Can you pay me in hot dogs?" James joked as Bert entered his office and took a seat. She held baby Jennie who was crying a bit as Bert slowly eased into one of the fancy brown leather chairs facing Miner's mahogany desk.

"Sure, as long as you bring Mayor McKay and Congressman Russo to lunch with you," Bert replied.

"I can't believe Jennie is two already. Adorable. Looks just like you, you know. So WGN is coming after your little business? I made a few calls after we spoke on the phone, and the executives at WGN don't want to cause you legal trouble. It would harm their reputation to be known as Big Brother coming after some small time business folk trying to start a fledging restaurant in one of the suburbs," James continued, now leaning back in his chair and sounding more and more like an attorney. "Their injunction was just a ploy to get your attention, and as long as you don't use the actual same name as the character Bozo the Clown on their television show, they'll leave you alone."

"Can we use a version of it, such as Boz?" Bert asked.

"Interesting. Sort of like a new soda company deciding to call their product Peps instead of Pepsi," James leaned back, looking up at the ceiling.

"Would you be trying to use anything else that could in any way be associated with Bozo the clown? Like their colors or his likeness or his image?"

"No. We've been using orange and yellow stripes all along, and planned to continue with these colors, and we have never used any clown images. Bob Bell, the real Bozo, wears red and white. But we want to place a small smiley face next to the name Boz, sort of as a play on words and to establish a friendly image for our restaurant."

"Are you sure you're not really just sticking your tongue out at WGN?" James laughed, then continued. "Let me study it a bit more. I'll get back to you later this week with my recommendations. I think your plan is probably the right way to go. Say hi to Donny for me. Feels like just yesterday we were at Thornridge High. Time flies."

Bert left James' office optimistic. She knew in her heart things would work out. As she walked toward her car she scanned the various businesses lining Chicago Avenue. The shops in downtown Dolton were a mainstay for the tight-knit community. Newman Drugs, Pepe's Tacos, Jarp's Shoes, Horney's Value Village. She knew every store and every owner, and they were all backing her and Donny's new business.

As Bert approached the car preparing to strap Jennie into her baby seat, she found herself catching her breadth and realized how tired she was. The work of getting the business running while raising four kids was not easy. She knew things would just get busier as the business blossomed. Keeping up with the food orders, hiring people to serve, and all the other related responsibilities would be challenging to manage.

As Bert buckled Jennie in and closed the door, she glanced up and a passing car caught her attention. She didn't recognize the pretty young girl driving, her long black hair mostly covering her face. But the passenger looked a lot like Donny. However, her mind was still on the meeting with Miner, and the car passed too fast to be sure. "Couldn't be," she murmured under her breath. *I'm so tired I'm not seeing straight.* She dismissed the image as absurd, and chuckled to herself as she pulled her car keys from her purse and slid behind the wheel. She pondered for a second on the increase in Donny's late nights out drinking with Al, but she trusted they were mostly talking about business, about the construction project. She dismissed her worries as silly as she pulled onto Chicago Avenue and headed home.

———————————————————

"Congratulations, Chris. You're number twenty-eight. Griffith, Indiana is hereby the home of the newest Boz franchise. Cheers!" Don raised his glass of champagne up high, careful not to spill any on his new Armani suit. High enough to clink the other glasses held by the group celebrating the opening of yet another Boz franchise. They had reserved the private room at upscale Peter Cavallini's Villa Nova Restaurant to dedicate the opening of the first Boz outside the Illinois border.

Chris Kramer, also an old classmate of Don and Al, had moved his family from Dolton to Griffith several years ago to work construction, and couldn't wait to start his own Boz restaurant. Now 1985 and at fifty years old, Chris was done with the early mornings and outside elements erecting pre-fab houses in the expanding northwest Indiana suburbs. With twenty-seven other Boz operations spanning the Chicago suburbs, he had a feeling that the Boz product would be a hit in Indiana too.

Don had kept in touch with Chris over the years as the Boz business became a success. Twenty-eight restaurants in fifteen years was amazing for what started as a pipe dream and a single little hot dog stand on the corner of a vacant lot. Now hot dogs were only one of many items Boz served. Polish sausage, Italian sausage with onions and peppers, roast beef sandwiches on French bread, bratwurst, nachos, milkshakes, and Hostess pies rounded out the menu. The Boz phenomenon swept through the Chicago area like a blizzard, and never slowed its pace.

Don pulled out of Cavallini's in his new Mercedes Benz. It fit nicely in the three-car garage of the new house he and Bert built on California Street in Dolton. It was only a ten minute ride to the Dolton store and the new car wash across from the original Boz which he invested in last year. He needed to stop at the Dolton store to pull some cash out for dinner with Tracie that night. They began dating just before Don's first council meeting when he was sworn in as a newly elected Dolton Trustee.

Don's friends and family had encouraged him to get involved in municipal governance because everyone in the town loved him. Don was reluctant at first, but he decided to throw his hat in the ring in order to help people with their issues. Plus he liked the attention he got from having the title of Trustee. Dolton's racial landscape was changing, and white residents were resolute in holding on to the town as it once was—predominantly white. So Don and friend Michael Peck formed the Concerned Party of Dolton as their political platform. Peck was sworn in as Mayor the same night Don was appointed Trustee.

As Don entered the original Boz, still on site where it was built fifteen years ago, and still where he and Al occasionally made cameo appearances, greeting their most loyal customers a few mornings each week, the kids working there stopped their goofing around and tried their best to look busy. Marlene greeted Don with a hug, and flirted with him a bit. Kurt asked Don if he needed anything to eat, while I tried to look busy cutting onions in the back. Just the night before we threw a big party behind the store after closing time, tilling the register for beer money, then skinny-dipping in Lake Piscateers behind the lot. Cooling off on hot nights in the lake behind Boz was a recurring theme for high school kids who staffed Boz, as was giving free food to their friends, having massive food fights around closing time, exchanging hot dogs for pizza with other kids who worked at nearby Giovanni's, and making out in the walk-in cooler. It was July 4th weekend, and the Boz crew was enjoying the splendor of the Dolton summer and all it offered.

Don entered his office after talking to us, and pulled two hundred dollars out of the safe. He wasn't picking Tracie up for another forty-five minutes, so he closed his office door and made a few calls. One was to my father.

"Listen David. All you need to do is make sergeant, then we'll appoint you as lieutenant, then assistant chief. Once you are in that position, we can appoint you chief through Peck's authority as mayor. No, you don't need any college education. Just study for the sergeant's exam and the rest will take care of itself." Donny hung up, and a minute later the phone rang. It was Bert.

"Are you coming home soon?" she said, the house in the background now much quieter with all the kids except 16-year-old Jennie having moved out.

"I got pulled into some resident complaints I need to meet with them about tonight. Don't wait up for me. But I need to get some sleep because tomorrow I promised to appear at the Dolton Carnival."

"Who is working our truck there? Do you need me to help?"

"I think Kurt and Leane. Nah, I think we're fine. See you later tonight."

Donny hung up feeling a little guilty about his half-truths with Bert. He attempted to rationalize his infidelities and double life, and the best he could settle on was that he still provided well for her and the kids, actually at a level better than most other parents in Dolton. They had money, they had a big house and nice cars. They got to eat at the nicest restaurants in the south suburbs and Chicago. He knew he would never leave Bert. So an occasional tryst wasn't all that bad.

Don put the cash in his wallet, locked the office and headed out. His dinner with Tracie would put him at ease. She was twenty-seven and didn't mind that Don was married and would never leave his family to start a life with her. Occasional dates, dinners, and the excitement of being with a powerful older man with money and a title was more than enough for her. And as popular and well known as Don was in Dolton, Chicago provided an easy escape for their rendezvous.

Don's phone rang at 8 in the morning, and it was Kurt calling from the store.

"Don, Leane called in sick so I don't know who will work the carnival with me today," Kurt said, as he cradled the phone between his shoulder and ear, using both hands to finish striping and cutting cucumbers at the store. He needed to hustle to get everything loaded into the truck parked outside Boz so he could get set up at Dolton Park on time for the carnival.

"Let me see if Jennie can cover. I'll be up there in a bit. Just get everything ready," Don instructed, then headed toward Jennie's room.

"Hey sweetie. Sorry to wake you. I can really use your help serving at the carnival today. I'll pay you double if you can bail your old dad out."

Jennie rolled over and rubbed the sleep from her eyes. At sixteen she was a great kid, daddy's little girl, beautiful and tall.

"Uh, good morning to you too. You don't need to pay me double, and I'm happy to help. Just don't ask me to drive that truck. I just got my license and I'm a little shaky with stick shift."

"That's my girl. Thanks sweetie, and I'll drive it over to the park for you and Kurt. I'm going to hop in the shower. Grab some breakfast and we're out of here," Don said, kissing her on the forehead before rushing to catch a quick shower.

Over time Don and Al got lots of requests to serve Boz hot dogs at area picnics and carnivals, so they converted a fleet of trucks into mobile vending vehicles. The size of bread trucks, these hot dog kitchens on wheels helped Boz cater food for all the biggest summer carnivals and outdoor events in the Chicago suburbs. The trucks were known as the Boz SWOT trucks.

I was serving a line of customers as Don and Jennie entered the back door of the store and began helping Kurt. As Kurt and Jennie finished loading supplies into the truck, Don filled the steam table in the truck with water and lit the burners so the water could come to a boil before arriving at the event. This always saved time on site, and maximized the time that food could be served to hungry, cash-paying customers.

"Kurt, we're short on buns. Take your car and stop by Hostess Bakery on the way. Pick up twenty packages of buns, then meet us at the park. Jennie will ride with me in the SWOT truck," Don said, then headed out the back door to avoid any conversations with customers up front.

It was only a twenty-minute ride to Dolton Park, but Don knew he would need to hustle in order to start serving food by the agreed upon time. He pulled out of the lot and onto Cottage Grove, then made a sharp right turn onto 142nd Street. He heard a loud crash then a scream in the back of the truck and quickly pulled over. The steam table had fallen over when he made the turn, and the boiling water was pouring onto Jennie's legs as she was trapped under the heavy metal cooker.

"Oh my God!" Don exclaimed.

"Daddy, help me! It burns!" Jennie screamed in pain, tears rolling down her cheeks.

With only shorts on and her legs exposed, Don could tell she was seriously injured. He struggled to pull the heavy steam table upright, causing more scalding hot water to pour over Jennie's already badly burned thighs. There was no time to turn the truck around, so he picked Jennie up in his arms and carried her back to the store a half a block up the road.

"Mike, call 911 and get an ambulance here now!" Don yelled as he burst through the front door cradling Jennie like a newlywed. Jim and Margie, working the store with me that day, were horrified by the sight of Jennie's bright pink legs, and ran to open the bathroom door so Don could carry her in.

"I'll get a bucket for cold water," Margie said. Don poured bucket after bucket of cold water on Jennie's leg's attempting to cool them down. But the pink flesh slowly turned to bright red, and with each new bucket of water more skin peeled off of Jennie's legs and washed onto the bathroom floor. The smell of her burning flesh consumed the store, an indescribable scent that competed with and overwhelmed the otherwise typical smell of boiling hot dogs.

The fire department arrived shortly after, followed by the crew from Daley's Ambulance, and began treating Jennie. We felt helpless as they worked on Jennie, and closed the store as she was loaded into the ambulance.

Don followed the ambulance to the hospital in a trance. *How could I have been so careless?* He kept picturing the scene in the SWOT truck over and over in his mind.

Jennie lay in the ICU for several days with second and third-degree burns. There would be months of treatments, skin grafts, and plastic surgery to correct the nerve damage and physical appearance of her legs.

———————————   —— —— —

"Hey babe. Do you need another pillow? Anything I can get you?" Bert asked.

Don shook his head no. It was November, 1998, and Sundays meant Bears games on television. He spent most days recently confined to his wheel chair and watching game shows, talk shows and even General Hospital on television. He couldn't wait for each weekend to roll around so he could turn on his favorite sport.

Only five years earlier it was all going well. As his successes as a businessman and as a Dolton Trustee continued, the buzz spread that Don would be the next Mayor of Dolton. He was humbled by the suggestion, and modestly said he wasn't sure he was ready, but he secretly hoped he might someday enjoy such a title. Then after Mayor Michael Peck died suddenly at the age of only 44 in 1993, Don was elected Mayor. As he promised, in 1990 he and Peck appointed Sergeant Dave Walker as Lieutenant, then as assistant chief in 1990, then Chief of Police in 1993. Don saw something in Walker that he trusted—a blue collar work ethic and can-do attitude, much like the values that made Don successful over the years. The Hygrade factory worker was the most powerful man in Dolton.

As he waited for kickoff of the game, he pictured vividly the day the call came from his doctor…Don had just wrapped up a big meeting at Village Hall when his secretary passed him the note: "Call Dr. Loew." He didn't think anything of it, and waited a few days to check in.

"Hello. Don here. Oh, hi Doc. Sure. I'll come in tomorrow afternoon. Okay. Thanks." Don remembered hanging up and thinking it was nothing. Some routine medical stuff. He was in his early sixties and in great shape. Everything in his life had gone right ever since Anthony Gilmartin purchased that first hot dog. He remembered the laughter that his and Al's family shared as they opened the little stand on the corner, as they prepared to build the first restaurant where Anthony's Produce once stood, and how Bert's visit to Kaiser helped jump start their customer base.

The phone call to Bert after his conversation with Loew was also still clear as day. "Doctor Loew called and said he has some concerns about my test results. He wants to see me tomorrow. What do you think?"

"Probably just a precaution. You were short of breadth at the house last weekend because you were out back splitting wood for three hours. Really, it's probably nothing. Want me to tag along?" Bert replied.

"No. I'll call you and let you know. I'm in great shape. It's nothing."

Then the words that came from Dr. Loew's lips that day in the doctor's office changed Don's life.

"Don, I regret to inform you, you have Amyotrophic Lateral Sclerosis."

"I have what?"

"ALS, also known as Lou Gehrig's disease."

Brown Funeral Parlor was packed. The men from Hygrade and their families, village officials, town residents, franchise owners and their staffs, Kaiser employees and other friends and family all came to pay their respects to Don, Donny, Mr. Hart, Mr. Mayor—whatever he was known as to each of them. All spoke kindly of the man who became an overnight success. The man who made it out of the factory and into Village Hall, the man who helped others find work, or slid them a few dollars to help them out. The guy who invented the best hot dogs in Chicago, and the guy Bozo the clown refused to smile for. The guy affectionately known as, the Hot Dog Man.

FEAR

"Erica, bring your dad another scoop of potatoes. Perfect, Stacy, just enough garlic in them this time."

"Daddy, you'd eat them whether they were perfect or not," Erica smiled as she walked toward the stove to add another scoop to her dad's plate. This made Frank smile and wink in Stacy's direction. Frank was a blessed man with a great new job, a beautiful wife and two great daughters.

"You've hardly touched your meal, Erica. Is something wrong at school?" Stacy said.

"Not at all. I'm just not very hungry lately."

Erica had just turned ten, and although she was diagnosed several years ago with slight anxiety disorder and obsessive compulsive tendencies, in most respects she was an average kid. Stacy and Frank never detected any signs of trouble with her eating habits before, so there wasn't cause for alarm about them now.

The Carlsons were a somewhat typical American family. Stacy and Frank met in college at Illinois State, then married after Frank finished graduate school at the University of Illinois with a degree in secondary education. He always wanted to be a high school principal. Stacy got her degree in business, having moved to Illinois from Indiana after her parents divorced during her senior year of high school. She missed her small town in Indiana, relatives and friends, but knew her life with Frank was going to be everything she dreamed of.

After taking a teaching job in Bloomington for several years, Frank got the offer to be principal at Thornridge High in Dolton, IL. He didn't know much about Dolton, but it was a Chicago suburb which meant plenty of opportunity for Stacy to find work, and an opportunity for them to settle in the Midwest. They would only be two hours from the friends they made at ISU and U of I, and less than three hours to Stacy's hometown of Lafayette, Indiana.

"Erica, I'm getting tired of telling you to finish your plate. Next time you'll sit there until it's all gone," Frank said to her. He recalled all the times he gave his parents fits about eating, and how they would make him sit at the table until "every last bit of your food is gone," as his mom recited on more than a few occasions. This usually did the trick, and he would begrudgingly eat his food in order to be excused. These recent spats about food with Erica felt much the same. Kids being picky and difficult about what they eat, though Erica used to enjoy anything they put on her plate. At ten, it seemed normal that kids would give their parents a hard time about food, he initially rationalized.

In the beginning, Erica's aversion to food went mostly unnoticed. A few scraps of chicken left here, barely any salad taken from her bowl, a glass of milk untouched there. And always the first to finish and leave the table, quickly discarding her leftovers into the trash and rinsing her plate clean. *I'll do it fast and mom and dad won't notice. They're too caught up in talking about work, the bills, Jamie and I starting school.*

The Carlsons usually served meals at home informally, buffet style. Stacy would place appropriate portions for the four of them on each plate on the island in the kitchen, then they would grab their plates and be seated at the nearby table.

Most people with kids might agree that it's hard to notice changes in your kids because you see them every day. So when Erica first starting losing weight, Stacy and Frank simply didn't notice.

After the table was cleared and the girls were tucked in, Stacy decided to broach the subject with Frank. "Is it possible at ten years old that she's dieting? I never thought ten-year-olds cared much about what they ate. When I was ten I ate everything in sight."

"I don't know. She was with your wacky sister at Delevan Lake this summer for a few weeks, and I noticed she came back talking about wanting to grow up to 'be a model.' Do you think something happened there that planted a seed with her about needing to lose weight?" Frank asked.

"Well Jane and I talked about this the other day on the phone, and she said Erica and her cousins mostly just went to the beach during the day, and at night they watched a lot of television including a show about modeling. Then they began pretending they were models walking down the runway, you know, just kids goofing around. But that was it," Stacy said, not trying to sound too defensive. *God I hope Jane didn't say anything to her about needing to lose her baby fat. Erica takes everything so literally, and is so willful,* Stacy thought to herself. But Frank was already going down that path.

"Why we would let your sister keep an eye on our kids without us being present is beyond me. In retrospect, that was a bad idea. I know we were getting settled here and everything this summer, but that woman could screw up a peanut butter and jelly sandwich."

As Frank spoke, Stacy changed into her pajamas and sat on the edge of the bed. She knew that he didn't care for her sister Jane much. She always took the easy way out to avoid any adult responsibilities or work of any kind, marrying a rich, older man, working for nothing. Stacy stood up and closed the door in case the girls were still awake upstairs. She didn't want them to hear the discussion that was about to unfold.

"Frank, that's not really fair. My sister was doing us a favor by taking the girls for a few weeks. I highly doubt Erica's skipping a few meals is related to anything that happened at the lake."

"Really? Well in case you haven't noticed, it isn't just a few meals. Watch her carefully over the next few days. She makes excuses about why she isn't hungry. She barely puts any food in her mouth, and she looks like she's lost ten pounds since she came back last month. She seems a bit overwhelmed lately. She's just not herself."

Frank's voice increased in volume and his typically calm demeanor was slipping away. This increased Stacy's agitation and she began adjusting the picture frames on her bureau, and re-folding the clothes on the chair at the end of the bed.

"Then we need to get strict with her. You know how bright she is. She overthinks everything and worries about anything. We just need to help her understand that skipping meals isn't healthy," Stacy said, mostly to convince herself of how to handle the situation, but now lost in worry, pacing from one corner of the room to the other and unconsciously manipulating every object in her path.

Stacy continued, now somewhat rambling, "It's not like we're terrible parents, right? We love our kids, we provide for them, we've never laid a hand on them. We aren't overly compulsive. We're not obsessed with our bodies or how we look. Lots of other couples stay in shape and their kids don't freak out about it. I mean, she's only ten years old. What are we supposed to do with her?"

Frank noticed she was coming a bit unglued, and approached her to provide some reassurance. Stopping her in her tracks in the center of the room as she paced, he embraced her with a hug that was as much for his own comfort as it was for hers. "It'll be ok," he said quietly in her ear. Then he leaned away from her, still holding her hands, and said, "We've always made things work, and this time will be no different. We've always been without family living near us, and everything has worked out fine."

Stacy woke the next morning less rested than usual. She had dreamt about furiously cleaning the house from top to bottom. Dusting, mopping, running the vacuum, scrubbing the baseboards and doing the windows. But in her dream, the harder she worked and the more she cleaned, the dirtier the house appeared. Her tireless efforts to clean were to no avail, and she woke feeling exhausted. This would be the day that she engaged in battle with Erica on the eating thing. *Today I'm going to get tough and put this nonsense to rest. I'm a good parent. I can handle this*, Stacy thought.

Stacy entered the bathroom and continued to talk to herself about the best approach with Erica. *I survived my parent's divorce. Mom's alcoholism. I moved from a farm in Indiana. I had no friends, then enrolled in a college where I knew no one. Then we up and moved to suburbia. If I managed all that, I can at least figure a way to make sure my kid eats.* "Small potatoes," Stacy said out loud to herself in the mirror.

Frank had already gone to work by the time Stacy entered the kitchen, and left one of his usual notes for her on the counter: "Have a good day, sweetie. Relax, everything will be fine. See you around six."

Stacy focused on the number six in the note. This meant they would be together for dinner tonight in case they needed to tackle things with Erica. Many nights Frank had functions at the school that prevented him from being home for dinner on time. In his first several months as principal he was intent on making a positive impression. If Stacy was going to address things with Erica tonight, she would need reinforcement. She crumpled the note and threw it in the kitchen trash bin and headed upstairs to wake the girls.

Jamie was the first to come down for breakfast, and plopped two chocolate pop tarts in the toaster oven. It was her morning staple before heading to second grade. Jamie was an even-keeled seven-year-old without a care in the world. Precocious and full of life and free-spirited, Jamie viewed the world with wonder and amazement. She wanted to be an actress when she grew up, so she often dramatized elements of her daily routine. Jamie and Erica were polar opposites. Erica would be the brain, the consummate introvert but the one with everything just in place, the type-A personality and straight-A student. Jamie would more likely be the class clown, a B-student but popular among her classmates and befriended by everyone she crossed paths with.

Stacy made a point to be in the kitchen when Erica came down for breakfast, but tried not to be too obvious about monitoring her. She began emptying the dishes from the dishwasher as Erica entered the kitchen and went directly into the pantry for her favorite cereal.

"Morning, Mommy. Why are you doing the dishes before work? You usually ask me to do them when I get home from school," Erica said as she grabbed the box of Kix and placed it on the kitchen island. Nothing got by her.

"I just figured I would get them done this morning for a change. How'd you sleep?"

"Great. We have a new art teacher that starts today and I hope she's fun. Her name is Ms. Lydon, and she is transferring over from a school in South Holland. Art is one of my favorite subjects, so I hope she knows her stuff."

Stacy wondered how a ten-year-old could remember such details and speak so eloquently. Where most kids would easily put such facts out of their mind and just show up to class, a new art teacher actually excited Erica. After all, Stacy and Frank were never serious students at that age.

Jamie chimed in from the kitchen table where she was decimating her pop tarts, attempting to eat them with a fork and knife. "I like art too. I might be an artist when I grow up if acting doesn't work out. But right now I'm having my last meal on the Titanic before we strike the iceberg. Don't I look like Kate Winslet?"

"You look like a dork. Shut up and eat your stupid pop tart," Erica said.

"Erica, don't speak that way to your sister. Both of you get moving so you don't miss your bus. I can't be late for work again," Stacy said while carefully studying Erica as she prepared her cereal. But it was as though Erica knew she was being watched, so she intentionally poured a healthy bowl of cereal and splashed in the milk before joining Jamie at the table.

Stacy was relieved. Maybe she and Frank were worrying without cause. Maybe Erica had just hit a rough patch the last couple of weeks and wasn't as hungry as usual. All kids go through cycles with their taste buds, right? She closed the dishwasher and returned to the master bath to finish getting ready for work.

Erica took two bites of cereal, then slid across the living room to listen outside Stacy's bedroom door to wait for the hair dryer to begin. This was her cue that Stacy would be occupied for at least another five minutes doing her hair. She headed back to the kitchen where Jamie was still pretending to be having her last supper on the grand Titanic.

"Sissy. Be a darling won't you, and please pass me the salt and pepper. My steak tartare is a bit bland this evening." Jamie said with a strange British accent.

Erica laughed, but said, "First, you're not English. Second you're not on the Titanic. Third, you don't need salt and pepper for a pop tart. You're so strange!" As Erica spoke, she picked her cereal bowl off the table, looked toward Jamie to ensure she wasn't watching, and emptied her remaining cereal and milk down the kitchen sink disposal. Stacy would never hear her flip on the disposal with her hair dryer running. This was one of many foolproof systems Erica employed to mask her avoidance of food. Each strategy was smooth, tactful, and effective. Mostly though, it was easy in a busy family of four to skip meals undetected. Between the rush of the morning and being without one's parents at school, cutting down on intake was simple.

Lunch at school was an easy meal for Erica to skip. Stacy always packed her lunches with care, including a juice box, turkey sandwich cut in half, sliced carrots and a granola bar. But the lunchroom was an under-staffed zoo. The few teachers and volunteers in the lunch room spent their time handing out straws and napkins, cleaning up spills and instructing the kids to quiet down. Making sure little girls finished their food was not on their list of things to watch for. So other than trying not to be too obvious in front of her friends, manipulating her lunch was no big deal.

Erica's lunch routine was always the same. Peel the crust off the sandwich, pretty standard for little kids, and then take exactly two bites of her sandwich, one from each side. This gave the appearance that most of the sandwich was consumed. Then eat exactly three carrot sticks, subtly sliding the others into a napkin while keeping eye contact with the girls at her table. And she always held the sandwich for much of the lunch period, until the other girls began packing up. Then she would discard the carrots and the remaining sandwich in the trash when her table was excused. On her way out of the lunchroom after her friends had dispersed, she would give Ben, a boy in her class, her juice box and granola bar.

Between skipping breakfast and lunch, by mid-day Erica was operating on fewer than 100 calories. But this didn't faze her. She was on a mission to be the thinnest, prettiest girl in the school. She recalled how complimentary her aunt Jane had been of her last month at the lake. How pretty she said Erica was, and how she could easily be a model when she grew up. But her aunt also emphasized how models have to work out regularly and watch what they eat. Erica began following these instructions before leaving the lake house to head back to Dolton, having run every morning with her aunt. Though they hadn't noticed Erica previously fixated on modeling, something happened during that summer that seemed to peak her interest. She was on a mission to be a famous model someday. And her quest of this vision had begun.

It was around two years earlier that the Carlsons knew Erica was different. Erica often appeared nervous, not comfortable around strangers, and fixated on cleanliness and routines. At her first sleepover for a friend's birthday party, the girls began channel surfing after her friend's parents went to bed. They watched a scary movie where a child's parents were abducted by aliens and replaced with parents who devised a plan to kill everyone in the neighborhood. The night after she returned from the sleepover party, Erica came into her parents' bedroom in a cold sweat.

"Mommy, are you my real mommy?" she said to Stacy from the foot of their bed. Frank was already asleep, but would soon wake to help handle the situation.

Stacy was up reading, and looked at Erica over the top of her book, at first without much attention. "Of course, sweetie. Why are you out of bed?"

"How do I know if you and daddy are real or not? What if you aren't?" Now Stacy gave more attention to Erica, noticing she was stark white and her hair was damp and sticking to her perspiring forehead.

"Erica, what's wrong with you? What are you talking about?" Stacy asked as she sat up straight in bed, alarmed. Before Erica could answer, she projectile vomited all over the end of the bed and began crying. Stacy sprang from the bed and Frank woke to the commotion and popped up to notice what was happening.

"Holy cow! What's going on? Erica, what's the matter? Are you sick?" Frank asked as Stacy led her into the bathroom. He grabbed a towel to begin cleaning the pool of vomit Erica had expelled all over their bed.

"No Daddy. I just had a queasy feeling in my tummy." This was the first of many similar situations they managed with Erica. From age six on, she intensely worried about things no six-year-old should ever give a second thought. While they noticed that Erica didn't engage in traditional play like other kids—no dolls or make-believe role-playing typical for kids her age—they figured she was just advanced in her development. She preferred reading books and playing board games (backgammon was her favorite, and she was starting to learn chess), or learning card games like euchre, cribbage, or spades. Her room was immaculate, and she was Mommy's big helper when it came to household chores. She even cleaned Jamie's room without asking. Everything had its exact place, which they found a bit abnormal but adoring.

On several occasions at night Erica would enter their bedroom, express her fear or concern about things like what she was going to be when she grows up, or how long she was going to live, and Stacy began keeping a paper bag next to her bed in case Erica began to hyperventilate. When she was eight, they decided to bring Erica to a psychologist for an initial evaluation.

Dr. Shanahan asked Erica some questions in front of Stacy and Frank, and then spoke to her in private. She then called them back in for her assessment, which she delivered in front of Erica.

"I know you are worried about Erica, but the good news is you did the right thing by coming in. I think it would be helpful for Erica to begin seeing me once a week to discuss some of the things she is worried about, and for her to begin taking an anti-anxiety medication. Probably Zoloft would be best. Erica is incredibly advanced for her age in terms of cognitive and verbal skills, and she has what I would call obsessive-compulsive tendencies. But this isn't entirely abnormal for someone with Erica's intelligence. She simply has too much going on in her little head for her to manage, which is creating the anxiety she displays with you at home and around bedtime," Dr. Shanahan smiled as she patted Erica on the head.

So at age eight, weekly psychotherapy began, which Stacy and Frank were intent on providing Erica. Whatever it took, whatever the cost, they were going to help their little girl get better. The queasy feeling Erica often described didn't subside, but she seemed to be less agitated and worried after taking the Zoloft a few weeks. They weren't necessarily thrilled with medicating Erica, but they presumed the experts knew what was best. One afternoon Frank accompanied Erica to her therapy, and experienced how very willful she could be.

Dr. Shanahan finished her session with Erica and then called Frank in to join them. "Frank, I have given Erica a homework assignment. I have asked her to go home and take some of her books off her shelf and scatter them around on her bedroom floor. Then to take some of her clothes off their hangers and loosely place them around her room. I've asked her to do this and then leave these items there for a few days without placing them back where they came from. I want her to test her ability to exist in an environment where a few things are out of place, and then come back next week and tell me how it went, focusing on how she felt about leaving things untidy. Erica, do you think you can do this?" Dr. Shanahan said, her hands evenly folded in front of her waistline.

"Sure. No problem," Erica replied, smiling broadly at the doctor. As Erica and Frank exited the medical building, he held her hand and stopped outside the front door, leaning down to meet her at eye level.

"Erica, I'm very proud of the progress you are making, and I know things are going to be fine. Mommy and I love you very much," he said, then hugged her tightly.

Erica accepted his hug, then replied, "I love you too, Daddy. And there is no way I am doing what that lady asked me to do with my books and clothes. Never." Erica didn't wait for a reply, leaving Frank in a catcher's stance alone on the sidewalk as she walked toward their car.

Frank made it home from school earlier than expected, so they sat down for dinner as a family promptly at six. As usual, Stacy placed the food on the island and filled each plate. Tonight was spaghetti and meatballs, Erica's favorite meal. Jamie informed the group she would be playing the role of Monica from the television show Friends at dinner tonight. This statement went unnoticed, as Stacy and Frank were intent on watching Erica's dinner habits, prepared to address things with consequences this time. They were up for the battle, a unified front. "How was school today, girls?" Frank began.

"Daddy, my new art teacher made us finger paint today! It was fun, but I'm in fifth grade. Finger painting? It's for kindergarteners," Erica said as she pushed the food around her plate.

"Maybe she was just trying to get you all on her good side by starting with a fun activity," Stacy said with a tone of optimism. As they all sat down, Frank continued to make conversation so it wouldn't be obvious they were focused on Erica's eating.

"Man, has it been busy at school lately. The PTA wants us to hire more security for the hallways and I just don't see how the budget can handle it."

As the conversation continued, Frank studied Erica's behavior. She would take a string of spaghetti and twist it on her fork, then put her fork down on the plate and take a sip of water (she subtly replaced the milk she used to drink with water several weeks ago), then dab her mouth with her napkin, lift the fork, and repeat this cycle several times. "I have to use the bathroom," Erica said as she stood up.

"Go ahead. But when you get back get working on your dinner before it gets cold," Frank said with a more commanding tone than usual. *I'm all over this situation. No problem.*

As Erica left the table, Stacy realized that this too was a new habit during meals. Erica would routinely need to use the bathroom once or twice during each meal. *Was she stalling, spending time hoping we would finish our meals and excuse ourselves so she could discard her meal undetected? Was she spitting her food out into the toilet? Or, worse yet, was she throwing up her food?* Stacy was overwhelmed by these thoughts and convinced herself not to jump to conclusions. She engaged Jamie in conversation about why she was so into Friends episodes lately, and Erica returned from the bathroom and sat back down.

"I'm not really that hungry tonight. I had a big lunch today and then we had cupcakes for Olivia's birthday fifth period," Erica said as she twisted her fork. At this point in the meal, Frank had counted that she had eaten only three forkfuls of spaghetti, each with only one or two strands.

"Erica, people are starving in this world. I won't have you wasting food. You will sit there and finish your food tonight if it takes you ALL NIGHT LONG," Frank said sternly, pointing his fork at Erica as he emphasized the last three words of his directives to her. Erica's mind started racing- *He doesn't understand that I'm dieting to stay in shape. Can't he see that I want to be a model someday? He's trying to trick me, trying just to control me. He would love me even if I was FAT! But I'm stronger than that.*

Stacy sat in silence, letting it all play out. She didn't want to overwhelm Erica right out of the gates by ganging up on her, so planned to play good cop to complement Frank's role of enforcer. "Sweetie, eat a little more of your pasta, please. We're concerned that you're skipping too many meals. You need your food for energy," Stacy said in a level tone while placing her hand on Erica's thin forearm. "Mom, I know what food is for. Really, I'm just not that hungry tonight. Please don't overreact."

By now Jamie took notice of the conversation and decided to jump in, as only a seven-year-old knew how, and possibly to deflect the attention from Erica and de-escalate the rising tension at the table. "I actually like to spin my pasta on a spoon and eat it like a true Pisano, like Uncle Mike does. Watch my technique, sissy."

"Jamie, focus on your food, and Erica will focus on hers," Frank instructed, not in the mood for Jamie's theatrics tonight.

A long silence ensued, during which Erica reverted to the previous routine of playing with her food and sipping her water. Frank could feel his temper flaring, a mix of panic and absolution that *he* was the parent, and his kid *will do as she is told* or there would be consequences. Stacy could feel the pressure building up in Frank, like a pot of water gradually going from simmer to a rolling boil. She didn't know what to say, so she stood and began clearing her plate. Then Frank erupted.

"Erica, open your mouth and put that food in and swallow, or I will do it for you. I'm tired of this bullshit. Eat your damn food!"

"Really, Frank, that's not how—" Stacy began before he continued and cut her off.

"You will sit there all night long and eat that pasta cold if necessary, every last bit of it, or for the first time in years I will put you over my knee and swat you good."

By now Jamie was crying but not speaking a word, sitting motionless and staring at her plate. *Sissy got caught not eating. Why is everyone yelling? It's just food.*

Stacy was aghast standing at the sink, but also speechless. Erica felt like a caged animal with no way out. She failed to do enough to convince them there wasn't a problem, and now she was cornered. Her brain stopped working and her body took over, issuing up the best defense mechanism it knew. She stood up, now crying and screaming, and began to hyperventilate.

"Mommy, I feel sick," she said while panting to catch her breath. She was now white as a ghost and convulsing for air, her hands on her knees like a weakened prizefighter, legs buckling and about to hit the canvass. Stacy came to her aid just as Erica threw up on the kitchen floor.

"Great. Is this how it's going to be?" Frank said, offering no sympathy or condolence.

"My God, Erica, what's wrong? Come on, let's go lie down," Stacy held her as they walked upstairs, leaving Frank to console Jamie and wipe up Erica's vomit, again.

As he tended to the kitchen, Frank was overwhelmed with acknowledgement and recognition of the gravity of the situation. It wasn't just a spell of skimping on some meals, and it wasn't just a phase. This was much more than that. This was much worse than what they originally thought. This was a willful course of action that Erica was set on, and he knew her well enough to know she wouldn't stop just because they said so.

Over the coming weeks as they took notice of Erica's eating habits and restricted intake, it occurred to them that the situation was similar to initially noticing someone who starts drinking too much alcohol. A few beers here, a few glasses of wine there, with increased frequency and occasionally having "a little too much." And in order not to be alarmed or show too much concern, the initial reaction by loved ones is typically masked in humor and light-hearted acknowledgement. Like spending initial holidays with Stacy's mom in Indiana after they just met. "Mom's had a little too much again. Time for bed, mom," was Stacy's standard line. But it was no joking matter, and it only got worse.

About a week after the spaghetti episode, a student on the track team scheduled an appointment with Frank. A black girl named Desiree, who wouldn't tell Frank's secretary why she wanted to meet with him. But when Desiree walked into his office, the reason for her visit was obvious. Frank's heart sank. Desiree was about six feet tall with bright eyes centered in dark and sunken sockets, visible through the pretty hair hanging over her face, but her cheek bones were sharp and pronounced on her face, as though they might protrude through her skin if she moved too fast. Her lips were dry and brittle, cracked and slightly bleeding in spots. She wasn't smiling. She looked desperate and sad. She looked like she was about to die.

"Good morning, I'm Principal Carlson. Thanks for coming in," he extended his hand and shook hers, alarmed by how skeletal and frail her cold hand felt. But he maintained eye contact and didn't let her see his shocked response to her condition.

She nodded her head but said nothing, initially, then started. "My teammates said if I didn't come speak to you they would tell my coach, so here I am. They're worried about me."

"What are they worried about?" he asked, though he already knew the situation.

"They think I have an eating disorder."

"Do you think they're right?" Recognizing this wasn't his area of expertise, Frank began to worry he might ask the wrong questions and somehow mishandle the whole situation.

"I'm thin because I train a lot. I've had the flu recently, but I think I'll be feeling better soon," she said, without making eye contact. The words were flat and monotone, but took great effort for her to expel from her throat. It appeared every action for Desiree required great effort. Her excuses reminded Frank much of Erica's litany of reasons she was not eating.

He saw Desiree's square shoulders piercing the warm-up jersey she was wearing, noticed her knee bones pointing through her sweat pants, and the bones in her hands and fingers looked like those of an eighty-year-old's. He struggled to differentiate between focusing on how to advise Desiree and sorting through his own worries about Erica. He hoped the strain of compartmentalizing the need to address both situations wasn't obvious to Desiree. He really wanted to be present for her. After all, she came to him for help, even reservedly. "Have you been to see a doctor? Have you considered that perhaps you do have an issue with proper eating?"

"No. I haven't been to a doctor. No, I don't think I have a problem with eating. Anyway, I promised I would come see you. Can I go now?"

Frank talked to her a bit longer, then had his secretary walk her back to class. Two days later Desiree's parents withdrew her from school, indicating they were moving to another town.

Frank was troubled by his meeting with Desiree, followed by her sudden departure. He drove home from work after learning of her withdrawal from school wondering how common eating disorders were. Was Desiree's appearance in his office just coincidental, or was this some bigger message that Erica was in worse shape than he thought? Was Desiree's condition where Erica would be heading if things didn't improve? Whatever the case, he resolved to dig in and learn more about eating disorders. Clearly, he needed this knowledge now for both personal and professional reasons. His interaction with Desiree stirred a curiosity which resulted in his immediately reading up on eating disorders—anorexia nervosa, restricted eating, bulimia nervosa, binge-purging, diagnosis, causes, cures.

The following weekend he took a trip to the local library to conduct his research. He consumed the information in chunks, ingesting the new knowledge with great hunger and excitement. There were hundreds of articles with more information and statistics than he could digest. After several hours of research he was exhausted but invigorated. Armed with more knowledge on the subject, he felt he would have an edge toward resolution. He printed a few articles to bring home to Stacy and left the library optimistic about where things were heading. He was always calm and positive, and things always worked out for them. He was always able to will his way through the tough times. If money was tight, he did side jobs to earn a little extra cash. If Stacy and he were drifting, he paid her a bit more attention. When grad school got tough, he studied harder. There was always a solution to every problem.

Two nights later, Frank was doing some touch-up painting in the downstairs hallway. The walls were already scuffed when they moved in, so a fresh coat of paint would conceal the black marks and make it look new again. He found himself more immersed in household projects lately, perhaps to help clear his mind and decompress. He finished up and remembered that Ridge was playing Thornton at seven, so they decided a night out would do them good. He could tell by Stacy's mood that Erica's disorder was weighing on her. Stacy's days had become a mix of tending to her work at a nearby real estate agency and worrying about Erica. While he approached the situation methodically, Stacy approached it intuitively. Her maternal instinct amplified her worry, and crystalized her vision of what was going on. Frank was able to do the math and help devise a strategy, but Stacy had an understanding of Erica's disorder that was beyond what she was experiencing visually. She instinctively knew in her soul that Erica was sick, and it twisted her heart like a tourniquet.

Frank cleaned up and he and Stacy headed out, arriving just before tip-off. Through all their stress and problems, they always found comfort in each other's company, and midway through the first half he reached over and held Stacy's hand. It appeared she was enjoying the game and relaxing. Then she turned to him and brought up the subject that was the very reason they needed a night away.

"Frank, do you think Erica is doing any better with her meals?"

"It's hard to say. She definitely is not eating like she used to. She's careful about not being too obvious around us, but I can tell she is focusing a lot on food and not eating much."

"She used to eat everything we prepared. Now she only eats certain items, and very small portions. I weighed her the other day and she is down ten pounds from the beginning of summer. That's a lot for a kid her size," Stacy fidgeted in her seat to see if their conversation was discernible to those sitting around them.

"We need to explain to her that if she doesn't work to get better we'll have to bring her in somewhere, and possibly leave her there for 30 days. I would hate to do it, but if it meant proper treatment I would," he stated, as the halftime show began.

The dance team took the floor to do their routine. Like many other high school dance squads, the Thornridge cheerleaders were cookie-cutter girls of lean physiques. Their squad also competed in regional tournaments, and had made a name for itself as one of the better cheer units in the South Suburbs. While they were all clearly in shape and had little body fat, one girl stood out visibly from the rest. She looked to weigh around eighty pounds at most, and her stick-thin legs looked as though they might snap at any moment.

Stacy noticed her first, and Frank could gauge from the expression on her face what she was thinking. Would this be Erica in a few years? Are we a society filled with girls who waste away to nothing? The distraction of seeing the girl spoiled their ability to focus on the rest of the game, so they left midway through the second half to stop at Nick's Tavern for a beer before heading home. Meanwhile, Jamie and Erica were with the babysitter from up the block, a community college student named Gina who had watched the kids already a few times since they moved into the neighborhood.

"Erica, I'm making your sister some popcorn, do you want some?" Gina shouted from the kitchen toward the living room where Jamie and Erica were on the couch watching television.

"Nah, I'll have something later. Thanks Gee."

"Ok. Suit yourself. I'm putting extra butter on it though. Are you ready for me to start the movie?"

Jamie was curled up under a blanket with her favorite pink pillow tucked under her arm. "Cool! I've been waiting to see March of the Penguins forever! Mom keeps promising to buy it. Thanks sooooo much for bringing it over."

"You know your Gee-Gee loves you guys. Erica, where are you going?"

"I just need to use the bathroom before we start." Erica headed into the bathroom nearest the kitchen and closed the door behind her. Jamie asked for more salt for her popcorn, so Gina headed into the kitchen. As she neared the hallway where the bathroom was, she thought she heard what sounded like someone getting sick from within. Something was wrong with Erica, she thought. Gina opened the door to see Erica on her knees with her head over the open toilet. Surprised that Gina walked in on her, Erica's head spun around and she quickly flushed.

"Erica, what's the matter? Are you okay?" Gina, startled, shouted as she approached Erica.

Erica had forgotten to lock the door, and stood up quickly, clearly surprised by Gina's presence. "I'm fine. I think I just have the stomach flu. I'm better now. You don't need to tell my mom and dad. They'll just worry." Erica flushed the toilet, leaned over the sink and rinsed her mouth, then walked past Gina and out of the bathroom.

When the Carlsons got home Gina simply told them she thought Erica wasn't feeling well. She never indicated she threw up, attempting to honor her promise to Erica and figuring it was just a flu bug of some sort.

The next day Frank decided to follow up with the athletic director to learn a little more about the dance team member's situation. The athletic director had no idea about the condition of one of her dance team members, what with all her responsibilities to run the entire department. But she agreed that as principal Frank should call the student, Maggie, in for a meeting. The meeting with Desiree wasn't smooth, and ended with her withdrawing from school. Frank wasn't looking forward to this meeting either. But before his meeting with Maggie, he decided to further bolster his knowledge on the subject. He stopped by to see the school nurse, Dr. Russ DeLuca. He liked Russ and respected his opinion.

Frank entered Dr. DeLuca's office and they shook hands. The handshake flashed him back to his recent meeting with Desiree, reminding him of how cold and bony her hand felt. Russ was fairly new to the school, but well-liked among the administration and faculty already. He was a unique and engaging guy who spent his evenings playing drums in a local cover band, The Trouts. Frank knew Russ would be someone who could give him some useful advice about eating disorders. "Hey Russ. How are things going this year so far?"

"Well, no cases of lice, only three reported pregnancies and only two cases of V.D. So by most accounts for a school of our size, I would say great," Russ retorted, motioning for Frank to have a seat.

"Look, I didn't deal much with students with eating disorders at my previous school, but I've already had one in my office here recently, and I expect to have another in any day now. I just don't want to misguide them. What's your take on how I can best help these girls?" he asked, reminding himself not to mention Erica. He didn't want to mix personal and business issues, but he obviously planned to apply whatever knowledge he gained from Russ toward dealing with Erica at home.

"Well, it's complicated. We live in a society that places so much emphasis on appearances. Our kids watch a lot of TV, and TV is full of beautiful people with slim bodies who look happy. Every other commercial on TV markets a new weight loss remedy or the latest piece of exercise equipment to give us 'rock hard abs.' So our kids are perpetually invaded with these images. Add to all this the peer pressure they feel in high school and college, and the stress of academics and other social pressures, and the result for many is the need to apply some locus of power and control over something. For some girls, this power comes from being able to control what they eat and how much. It's something they can accomplish, and the by-product is, they look good. But then it takes hold of them and they can't stop."

"So it's not necessarily psychological then?"

"For some there are deeper-seated issues that result in eating disorders. Early trauma or abuse, or even depression, or OCD-related diagnoses can be related to eating disorders. It really just depends on each person." His mention of OCD gave Frank pause, though he continued to focus on his words without registering any alarm.

"Look at it this way," Russ continued, "an eating disorder is a lot like an addiction, except inverted. Much like the alcoholic who refuses help until they hit rock bottom or experience a successful intervention, a person in the early stages of an eating disorder will typically be in total denial about the severity of the situation. Either because they see themselves as overweight when they're not, or simply because they believe they can control it and turn it on and off when they want to. Just as alcohol stimulates the pleasure center of the brain making drinking more attractive to the drinker, the power that comes with being able to control one's body by not eating also becomes as intoxicating as liquor. Perhaps more so, because the high it produces comes in the intense power felt by controlling one's body and losing weight."

Russ continued, now seated across from Frank and totally engaged in the topic at hand. Frank was relieved that Russ knew a thing or two about eating disorders. "But to appreciate the power of denial, we must think about how we would react if someone wanted to take our most cherished possessions from us. A nice car, our house, our beloved pet, our wife or child. How we would be if someone came to us and said, 'Sorry. You can't keep it any more. It's mine.' In the mind of an addict, this is the thought process that occurs. Admitting I have a problem means I have to change. Change means I will lose what I cherish more than anything in this world. The booze. The hit of crack. The line of coke. The ability to control staying thin. The power to keep from being fat. Some girls would rather die than give it up. And every year many do."

"This all makes sense," Frank replied, his mind swimming with all that Russ had said. Erica, Desiree, Maggie. What was causing their specific inability to eat, and how could they be cured? How bad was it for Erica, and what could Frank possibly do to help?

"The average American gains forty pounds between the ages of twenty and forty, and six out of ten Americans go on a diet at least once each year. For some, dieting becomes obsessive if not dysfunctional. Eight million Americans suffer from an eating disorder, seven million of them women, and one of every two hundred American women suffers from Anorexia Nervosa, including four percent of college women. Early intervention is the key."

As Russ provided some of the basic facts and figures, he reached onto his side table and pulled a flier off a stack and handed it to Frank. He read aloud the heading before returning his focus to Russ: "The Facts About Eating Disorders."

"Refer students to me first, and I will get these cases in front of our health management team for discussion. Success in helping these kids is dependent on their willingness to get help, and to participate in therapy, nutritional education, and, for some, anti-depression or anti-anxiety medication. We also typically involve their parents since most are minors. Eating disorders are long-term, so we need to catch them early."

A bit overwhelmed with all the information, Frank shook his head in agreement. His time with Russ was well spent, but he didn't want to exploit his time or appear totally novice in his knowledge on the subject. As he stood up to see himself out, Russ' last statement resonated with him the most.

"Whatever you do, don't underestimate how powerful eating disorders are, and how dangerous. Medical complications ranging from organ failure to heart trouble can result if untreated. Remember, when a girl with an eating disorder looks in the mirror, the image is distorted. While you and I may see a beautiful person that needs to gain a few pounds, the person with disordered eating sees someone grossly overweight who needs to shed fifty pounds. And if this same person has the will to do it, the result can be fatal."

As Frank walked back toward his office he began reading the brochure Russ had given him. He scanned the page and several phrases caught his attention:

"Disordered eating -- The clinical term for eating disorders such as anorexia or bulimia, is a *disease*. Like coaxing an addict to stop drinking or using drugs, it almost always requires much more than encouragement, pleading or even threats. While an alcoholic drinks and a drug addict uses drugs, an anorexic restricts eating to compensate for issues or problems they are dealing with. Until the primary causes of the dysfunctional behavior are rooted out with professional intervention, the behavior usually continues. Unlike a broken arm that needs only time and stability to heal, people suffering with and recovering from eating disorders may require a range of applied treatments, combining psychotherapy, medication and nutritional education in order to resume a functional lifestyle. Detection and treatment of eating disorders in their initial stages stand a high likelihood of successful intervention and treatment, although many eating disorders are long term."

Frank assumed that Erica was in the initial stages of the disease, and worried that the negative behavior was already fueling itself into a powerful force that was getting stronger and stronger, like a campfire that starts with a few twigs and sticks and takes on a life of its own. A life that must be managed either by adding fewer logs to contain it, or more logs to make it bigger and hotter. But some campfires burn out of control, hungrily consuming everything in their path. He worried that Erica's fire was burning that way, her eating disorder taking the form of its own entity within her, taking over her body and mind.

Erica sat in school sizing everyone up, placing each person into the tidy little printer's rack in her mind. This person is smart, this person is strong, this person is pretty, this one is thin, this one fat. And in doing so, she constantly measured herself against what she saw... *I'm smarter than Taylor but not as smart as Katy. I'm thinner than Stephanie but not as thin as Morgan.* She spent a lot of time fixated on how to be smarter, prettier and thinner than all the other girls. She applied a great deal of energy toward improving in each category, and trying to come out on top.

Maggie, a senior, came into Frank's office the next day, and he flashed back to his recent meeting with Desiree. There were some differences, though. While Desiree seemingly concocted the story of having the flu to match her symptoms and behaviors, Maggie was much smarter. She claimed to suffer from a hereditary disorder that doubled her metabolism, making it impossible to gain weight even though she consumed double the calories of other kids her age. She didn't look as depressed as Desiree, but she was strikingly thin. Frank described to Maggie the resources that the school offered to students with health issues, including eating disorders, and asked her to check in with Russ as soon as possible for a checkup. Maggie agreed, smiled, and left his office.

Frank called down to inquire about Maggie with her dance coach, who reported that she was a kid everyone liked and seemed to be doing fine. The coach said Maggie was the same size and weight now as when she started with the team as a sophomore. Frank pulled Maggie's grades and was impressed to see she was earning nearly all As. Then he checked with the staff down in the training center where the athletes work out after school, and asked that they keep an eye on her. They later reported that Maggie came into the center every day, wore extra clothing to sweat more, and worked out on the cardio equipment vigorously and usually without hydrating herself. It wasn't uncommon for athletes, including girls on the dance team, to do intense daily workouts at the center, but the layers of clothing and lack of water during exercising was concerning.

Frank knew Maggie was a time bomb waiting to go off. He suspected, based on his meeting with her, that she wasn't getting treatment for an eating disorder, because she didn't believe she had one. Moreover, he knew she was practicing dangerous behaviors for a kid of her size, roughly eighty pounds and pushing her heart to its limit every day. He was afraid she would die working out, on his watch and under his responsibility as principal. He decided to up the ante and called her parents to discuss the matter with them. Much to his surprise, her family defended her and said they would take care of it "outside of school." The threat of removing her from the dance team also had no impact.

Frank was running late to get home. It was 6:30, and he already missed dinner even though Stacy begged him to be home on time. He packed his stuff into his brief case to head out, and once in the car and on the road gripped the steering wheel tightly. Between the stress of the job and Erica's situation, he was feeling more pressure than he was accustomed to managing.

When he walked in the door, he knew immediately there had been an incident. Jamie was upstairs with her television on and door closed. He heard crying through Stacy's door, and Erica sat alone at the dinner table, all plates and glasses removed except hers. As she turned to acknowledge his arrival, Frank could see for the first time how bad things had become. His little girl was wasting away. She was no different from the girls he was dealing with at school. Just younger and smaller and, for the first time, he could tell she was scared. Frank was no longer worried. He was terrified. He tried to hide his emotions, and approached Erica as calmly as possible.

"Hi sweetie. Where is everyone?" he asked.

"Jamie ate fast and went to her room to catch Friends re-runs. Mom and I had a fight and I think she is crying. Daddy, do you think I'm going to die?" He dropped his bag and approached Erica and pulled up the nearest chair.

"Of course not sweetie. Well, sure, at some point, like the rest of us. What are you worried about?"

"Mom said if I don't eat I'll die."

"Well that's true. Are you having trouble eating enough?"

Erica sat still and looked down at her stomach, which was impossible to see under her loose tee shirt. Frank rested his hand on her arm and knew that if he closed his hand that his thumb and index finger would easily touch around her forearm with room to spare. Erica's lips were parched and dry. "Baby, have a sip of water, please. I can tell you're dehydrated by looking at your lips."

Erica grabbed her water glass and took a small sip, a concession she knew carried no consequences in terms of calories. "Why do you think you can't eat?" he asked.

"I'm just not hungry. Nothing tastes good anymore."

"But you need food to fuel your body. You know that, right? In that sense, Mommy is right. We need food, water, and sleep to stay alive."

"Mommy said if I get sent to the hospital they will jab needles in my arms and feed me through a tube connected to my tummy. Then she stopped talking and started crying and left."

"Well Mommy cares about you. So do I. Do you want something else for dinner instead of chicken and carrots?" Frank could see she pushed the food around on her plate, but doubted she had consumed any of it.

"Can I have a bowl of cereal?"

"Sure. Daddy will get it for you."

"No." Erica quickly jumped up. "I'll get it, Daddy. You just got home from work so you need to get your dinner too. We can eat together, ok?"

Erica went to the pantry to retrieve her favorite cereal, placed a bowl on the counter, and reached in with her hand and grabbed a handful of cereal and placed it in the bowl. This action went unnoticed by Frank, as he wasn't around enough at breakfast to be familiar with Erica's breakfast habits. But Erica's mind guided her calculated movements with precision. Only one handful of cereal, she told herself. *This will be enough for dinner, with a little milk, to fill my tummy and make Daddy not worry. But only one handful and not a bit more.* Erica returned to the table where Frank placed his plate of food and had started eating.

"Daddy, what I said before about not being hungry really isn't exactly true. I think that I actually am hungry, but it feels like I am just afraid to eat. I think I'm getting fat, and I'm worried if I eat I'll just get fatter."

"I know sweetie. This is why you need to keep seeing the doctor. But they said if you don't gain at least a few pounds they have no choice but to have you go somewhere for a month on your own. Without me and mommy and sissy. You don't want that, do you?"

After dinner Frank cleared the table and walked Erica up to bed. He told her he would be back to tuck her in later, and headed to the bedroom to check on Stacy who hadn't emerged since he arrived home.

Stacy was lying on her side, reading the latest Danielle Steel novel. They talked about his conversation with Erica, and about his conversation with Russ. Stacy felt relieved that Erica acknowledged the danger of not eating. That she had a bowl of cereal also helped to calm Stacy a bit.

"Russ DeLuca was very helpful. Some of what we discussed I already knew. But he put things into perspective. He compared an eating disorder to an addiction. I never thought of it that way. But when we first noticed Erica's pattern of eating less, it did seem a lot like initially noticing someone who starts drinking too much. Sort of like dealing with your mom. A few beers here, a few glasses of wine there. Then it just snowballs and gets out of control. Just like skimping on meals. First it's just skipping a portion here and there, and next thing you know it's a full-blown aversion to food."

Frank continued, seeing he had Stacy's attention given he was speaking on behalf of DeLuca, a professional with expertise in the area of eating disorders.

"When we were initially dealing with your mom's alcoholism, we had no idea how to manage it. If you've never been around someone with an addiction, you have no sense of how to properly manage the situation, right? I mean, you can't. It's like trying to speak a different language with no training. If you've spoken English all your life, you don't wake up one morning and start speaking Portuguese. It doesn't work that way."

Frank caught himself carrying on a bit, and stopped to check in with Stacy. She sat Indian style on the bed, legs crossed with her back against the headboard and hands clasped in her lap. Her tears had dried, but she looked intensely worried, like a student sitting in class about to be asked an important question by the professor for which she has no answer to give. But Stacy attempted to articulate what she was thinking at the time.

"It just feels like we're fumbling things. We're saying all the obvious parental things that we hope will work. I've begged her to eat, I've threatened to punish her if she doesn't eat, and nothing works. But mostly I am afraid our little girl feels trapped inside some horrible monster, his arms tightly wrapped around her body and she is terrified that she can't break free. I mean, imagine how a ten year old must feel dealing with this. It's mind numbing, and it's just not fair."

"I know," he agreed as he took a seat on the edge of the bed near her. "The other night we told her she would sit there until every bit of food on her plate was gone, and she sat there for two hours sipping her water. It's so frustrating, because we can't make her eat, but we know if she doesn't she is going to waste away. It's like when her therapist told her to let her room be messy for a few days and she refused to do it."

"It's common for family members of an addict to assign blame. I have asked myself a million times in the last week what we may have done to cause this. Where did we go wrong? How do we fix this? But it's not that easy. Erica put it into perspective for me earlier this evening. She used the word 'afraid' to describe her reluctance to eat. She isn't not eating because she isn't hungry. She can't permit herself to eat because of fear."

Erica hit rock bottom when, at age 12 in 7th grade, she got on the scale and weighed only 68 pounds. The psychologists and nutritionists working with her threatened to stop seeing her unless she gained weight or checked herself in to an in-patient facility.

"Erica, the doctors have told us we need to bring you to a special hospital for a month. I don't think we have any choice, sweetie," Frank said, as Stacy and he sat on her bed after they returned home from her weekly appointment. Her eyes were sunken in her face, and her thin frame was difficult to look at. She was withering away before their eyes. Stacy was crying, but not saying much at first.

"Daddy, don't make them do that. They'll stick needles in me and I'll be there all alone."

"We'll be there every day. Your health is more important than anything, and if you keep restricting they say you will damage your heart, and you may even die. Do you understand what I'm saying?" Frank looked directly into her face to see if she was absorbing what he was saying to her. She looked down at her hands folded in her lap, then replied, "I understand, but I have been trying..."

Stacy interrupted- "Erica we don't know what else to do. You're drinking three Boost shakes a day just to give you enough vitamins and nutrition to keep you upright. You refuse to eat, and you're so frail I'm afraid to hug you. This disease is killing you, and it's killing this family. Please snap out of it and take charge..."

"I am taking charge, Mommy. I'm trying the best I can."

"Then it's not good enough. It's time for you to be admitted. We don't have any choice. You have one week to show positive weight gain or your father and I have no choice than to check you in to a facility."

The thought of needles always petrified Erica. Ever since she was a kid she hated any doctor's visit involving needles. Even a routine shot or blood work freaked her out. This very likely was what helped her get on track. The thought of someone puncturing her and sticking an I.V. into her every day was just the vision that motivated her to begin eating. Her fear of needles was the determining motivating factor for her to get back to normal eating, just as fear of food was preventing her from eating to begin with. It was slow at first, but she eventually made enough of a weight gain that the doctors agreed to continue to see her on an out-patient basis.

By the time Erica was a freshman in high school, she had a great group of friends. She and the three other girls were thick as thieves. The Carlsons hosted them for sleep-overs, they went to movies together, shopping, and did the sort of stuff that teenage girls are supposed to do. The bond with the group was good for Erica. It gave her the support she needed as she confronted her demons in the kitchen, and at the dinner table. She was still underweight for her age and height, but she was out of the danger zone. Then one day Frank came home from work to find Stacy on the front porch, sipping a glass of wine.

"Hey babe. How was your day?"

"Fine until I checked the mail. Here," she handed him the letter.

"Mr. and Mrs. Carlson, we're really sorry but we don't know what to do. Erica won't listen to us about eating more, and last weekend we caught her making herself throw up. We're really scared for her, and just wanted to let you know."

It was signed by her three best friends.

"Man, just when we thought we were making progress," Frank said putting his stuff down and plopping into the chair beside Stacy. He could tell she had been crying.

"I guess we need to talk to her again. She always denied that she purged, but all those trips to the bathroom in the middle of meals out at restaurants. They always made me suspicious," he said, reaching for a sip of Stacy's wine.

"I already talked to her. Frank, do you know she throws up in the shower? She admitted she started purging when she was in seventh grade."

"Let's think about increasing her therapy visits, and possibly adjusting her meds. There must be something else we can do to help her that we haven't thought of."

"Daddy, I have to go the bathroom," Erica whispered.

"We're about to line up for communion," he whispered back. "Go through the line for communion, then use the bathroom and we'll meet you in the lobby afterward."

Stacy looked disgusted as usual, but didn't say anything. After six years of it, what else was there to say that hadn't already been spoken ten times? Jamie fidgeted in her seat a bit but was mostly unaffected. She too had developed an ability to tune it out upon demand.

"Daddy, I have to go *really* bad," Erica said, this time louder than a whisper, placing her hand on her skirt over her lap while bouncing in the pew.

"No! Chill out and wait five minutes!" he said, this time above a whisper and audible to others seated in their row.

Frank kept a calm facade but was boiling inside. Christmas Eve her sophomore year and she pulls this crap. Can't even put a damn pinch of bread dunked in grape juice in her mouth without freaking out. *When will this shit end?* he wondered.

As Stacy stood to file toward the front of the church for communion, Frank noticed for the first time in a while how she was aging, perhaps more rapidly under the circumstances. The constant worry was taking its toll on her, as were the trips to the doctors for Erica's blood work and labs, the monthly meetings with the psychiatrist and weekly meetings with the psychologist. Buying and preparing special meals and vitamin supplements, and the back and forth on what to eat and how much, not to mention the medical bills, were wearing her out.

In the car ride home from church Frank did his best to mask his frustration. Erica, now sixteen, was still contending with her eating disorder, though differently from when she was ten. After years of therapy she could openly discuss what was bothering her, and she typically ate fuller meals as long as she got to select the food and portion size. There were signs of progress and periods of regression. A good meal at breakfast might be followed by restricting her lunch to a few carrots, which might be followed by eating a full plate at dinner. Other nights she would skimp at dinner, then have two bowls of cereal before bed. The doctors openly discussed the disease with the entire family, Jamie included, to help them understand and cope with what Erica was going through. There would be good days and bad days. Restricting, binging, purging, and everything in between.

At the appropriate point in the drive home from church, Frank raised the question he was dying to ask. "Sweetie, why didn't you want to take communion? Was it the calories in the bread and juice or something different?" He reached over to hold Stacy's hand.

"Dad, it's no big deal. I just didn't want to wait in line to go up for it tonight. It's not like we're really religious anyway. I mean, we go to church on Christmas Eve and Easter, and a few times in between."

"I just don't want you to go backwards, that's all. You've made good progress recently, and your mom and I want it to continue. In a few years you are off to college, and I need to feel you can manage this on your own."

"Yeah, dad. I know. Thanks for your concern. I'm fine," she said defensively.

Over the years of dealing with Erica's eating disorder, they attempted to draw a balance of challenge and support with her. They complimented her when she ate a few good meals, and registered the usual concern when she skimped. While Erica was considered out of the danger zone in terms of her weight, she was still smaller than most kids her age. Six years of depriving herself of regular meals with the proper mix of food groups stunted her growth in a way that was obvious and permanent.

Stacy and Frank had grown accustomed to managing the situation. It was a bit like raising a child with a physical disability. Regular trips to the psychologist and nutritionist, lab work to check her blood and electrolytes, EKGs to check her heart rate, blind weigh-ins. They watched Jamie for signs of stress given her proximity to the whole situation, but she remained pretty resilient. They talked openly about things with friends and family, not wanting it to be a dirty secret kept in the appendix of the family journal. Erica was an amazing kid with a bright future, just wired differently and needing special guidance and nurturing.

The holidays that year passed, and it was early February when the letter came. Frank parked his car after work and walked to the end of the driveway to grab the newspaper and mail. It was cold out, but a beautiful light snow was falling.

The return address on the label wasn't familiar—Stephanie Strickland…Riverdale, Illinois. *Strickland?* He didn't know any Stricklands, but the letter was addressed to him and included his work title—Frank Carlson, Principal, Thornridge High. He opened it and read the letter before heading into the house:

Dear Principal Carlson,

My husband and I thought you would want to know that Maggie passed away several days after Christmas. Only 19 years old, she fought hard to overcome her long battle with anorexia, and in the end couldn't overcome it. She had some good months since graduating from Thornridge, and we appreciate that you tried to help her while she was a student. We recently placed her in an in-patient facility in an effort to save her life. Still refusing to eat, they placed her on intravenous feeding tubes just to keep her alive. We were at her side as a family as she slipped away. God has another little angel in heaven.[3]

Sincerely,

Stephanie Strickland

Frank pondered whether to show the letter to Stacy, and elected to put it aside until the appropriate time. He folded the letter and envelope and stuffed them into his coat pocket, exhaling a plume of crystallized breath into the cold night air. And through the falling snow he looked up to see Erica in her bedroom window looking down at him. The hand connected to her thin silhouette blew a kiss in his direction and waved, then faded away.

---

[3] This aspect of the story is embellished. No Thornridge student associated with this story died as a result of an eating disorder.

Zeus gave the beautiful box to Pandora, and asked her to admire it but not look inside. But her curiosity got the best of her, and when she opened it all the evil known to man sprang out and inherited the Earth. Pandora was struck with fear, but she looked at the bottom of the box to see a single word inscribed, and her faith and confidence were restored- HOPE.

CPSIA information can be obtained at www.ICGtesting.com
Printed in the USA
LVOW070534280213

321991LV00009B/260/P